"I don't always pig out like this, Michael, but I'm just used to eating at certain times, and it's late," Meghan said lightly.

"I'm just afraid you'll explode all over the place," he teased. "Where do you put it?"

"I have a hollow leg."

Michael's eyes grew wide in mock wonderment. "Which one?"

Meghan pointed to her left leg, then realized her error. He lifted the leg and placed it across his lap, rapped on it with his knuckles, then ran his hands up and down, sending waves of tingling excitement through her body. "This is incredible, a work of art. Looks perfectly natural and no hollow sound." He brushed his hands lightly over her calf and regarded her with interest. "Do you have any other secret hiding places? Your arm?" he suggested, running his fingers down its length. "Or your head?" he asked, placing his hands on either side of her face.

She was powerless to stop him, mesmerized by the spell he was weaving. Her most precious wish lay exposed in her eyes, that he make love to her tonight.

Michael struggled for control as he said, "Are you sure? I hear a rattle when you shake your head." He pressed his lips gently, sensuously to hers, savored the taste and feel of her. Meghan returned his kisses, each feeding the fires in the other until they were panting from the raging tempest they had created. . . .

WHAT ARE *LOVESWEPT* ROMANCES?

They are stories of true romance and touching emotion. We believe those two very important ingredients are constants in our highly sensual and very believable stories in the *LOVESWEPT* line. Our goal is to give you, the reader, stories of consistently high quality that may sometimes make you laugh, sometimes make you cry, but are always fresh and creative and contain many delightful surprises within their pages.

Most romance fans read an enormous number of books. Those they truly love, they keep. Others may be traded with friends and soon forgotten. We hope that each *LOVESWEPT* romance will be a treasure—a "keeper." We will always try to publish

LOVE STORIES YOU'LL NEVER FORGET
BY AUTHORS YOU'LL ALWAYS REMEMBER

The Editors

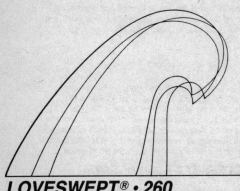

LOVESWEPT® · 260

Mary Kay McComas
Divine Design

BANTAM BOOKS
TORONTO · NEW YORK · LONDON · SYDNEY · AUCKLAND

DIVINE DESIGN

A Bantam Book / June 1988

*LOVESWEPT® and the wave device are registered
trademarks of Bantam Books. Registered in U.S. Patent
and Trademark Office and elsewhere.*

*If you would be interested in receiving protective vinyl
covers for your Loveswept books, please write to this address
for information:*

Loveswept
Bantam Books
P.O. Box 985
Hicksville, NY 11802

ISBN 0-553-21903-0

Published simultaneously in the United States and Canada

*Bantam Books are published by Bantam Books, a division
of Bantam Doubleday Dell Publishing Group, Inc. Its trademark, consisting of the words "Bantam Books" and the
portrayal of a rooster, is Registered in U.S. Patent and
Trademark Office and in other countries. Marca Registrada.
Bantam Books, 666 Fifth Avenue, New York, New York
10103.*

PRINTED IN THE UNITED STATES OF AMERICA

O   0 9 8 7 6 5 4 3 2 1

To Doss with love
For K.M.N.B.
And a special thank you to Pete.

One

Meghan finished applying her makeup and stepped back to study herself critically in the mirror. With her body bathed, lotioned, powdered and perfumed, her hair french braided and coiled skillfully at the nape of her neck, she was well satisfied with her efforts.

The outfit she'd bought especially to wear this evening lay on the bed. Over black silk string bikini panties she fastened a matching black garter belt and carefully pulled on dark silk stockings. Braless, she tied a black satin halter top around her neck and again behind her at her waist. Although the garment was completely backless, the front had a gently draped cowl neckline and appeared from that angle to be a nice, conservative blouse, perfectly suited to wear with her cinnamon-colored crepe dirndl skirt and jacket. Next she donned a pair of large, round nonprescription glasses.

Surveying the results in her full-length mirror, Meghan almost crowed with delight. In her one-inch pumps she looked ready to *do* business with a judge. If she took off the glasses and jacket, let down her hair, and put on higher heels, she'd look ready to *give* him the business.

Stuffing her extra pair of shoes and a clipboard, which held a hundred copies of her questionnaire, into her oversized shoulder bag, she took one last glance at herself in the mirror. Finally she grinned stunningly and winked at her image. With an anticipatory bounce in her walk, Meghan Shay set out to get pregnant.

In the cab, Meghan felt unexpectedly calm. It wasn't as if she did this every day. Maybe her confidence sprang from her conviction that what she was about to do was right for her, that the plan she had hatched had been years in development. She knew she wasn't being impulsive. It was a deliberate, well-thought-out, logical act. At least *Meghan* thought so.

She would have preferred to do this in the conventional manner. She knew hers wasn't the easiest way, but her heart was possessed by the idea. Meghan felt driven to take matters into her own hands. It was strange, she thought, the way you could affect your own destiny at times, and at other times fate took over. Then no matter how you tried to change things, you couldn't gain control.

In their most unrealistic moments of daydreaming she and Carl had planned to have a dozen children. They had finally settled on having three or four babies, to be started immediately after their "I do's," the day after graduation from law school.

Meghan shook her head regretfully. It still didn't seem fair that Carl's life had been cut short. Not just because of how it had affected her, but because Carl had been a kind, gentle, loving man. A good man, who could have had the world by the tail, if he'd only had the chance. Meghan still missed him and probably always would.

Years later she had fallen in love with Bob, a wonderful man who had much in common with her, except the desire to have children. When he proposed marriage, Meghan had been truly upset because she'd had to refuse, but she knew she wanted a child at least as much as she'd wanted him.

Her experiences with Carl and Bob were now arguments in favor of what she was doing. Life was short and it gave no guarantees. Meghan had come to learn that very few things in life were just given to you. Getting what you wanted called for effort and determination, for total control of your own destiny.

At the age of thirty-four, Meghan had decided not to wait for another man to come into her life. Time was passing and there was no assurance that he'd show up before her biological clock ran down. She desperately wanted a child. She had everything to give, and her heart told her it was time to take action.

"Have you considered seeing an exorcist before you get carried away with this plan of yours?" Lucy, her best friend and only confidante had asked after hearing Meghan's grand scheme.

"For heaven's sake, Lucy. All I want is one little sperm with some decent chromosomes. Is that so much to ask for?"

"No," she had conceded, "but have you thought about the man's right to know about his own child?"

"Give me a break, Lucy," Meghan had said vehemently. "Men run all over New York dropping their seeds indiscriminately. Exceptionally 'nice' men will take a woman to bed and just assume she's taken care of protecting herself and never even ask. So what if one of those seeds falls on fertile soil? Do you think the man will even think twice about the possibility? That's why he has to be a stranger. Preferably one from out of town. He'll drop his seed, leave town, and think of it as a fling at a convention in New York City." She paused briefly, then added in a gentler tone, "I don't want to hurt anyone, Lucy. I just want a baby. If I were honest with a man and asked him to please impregnate me, he'd turn and run like hell, thinking I wanted to make some sort of claim on his life. But if he thinks he's just getting a nice roll in the hay for free, if he never knows I'm pregnant, how could it possibly hurt him?" She had finished, making the whole outrageous idea sound simple.

"There's got to be a flaw in there somewhere. I just don't hear it yet," Lucy had replied. "Give me some time to think it over."

"You have till Saturday," Meghan had warned.

Lucy had called several times to voice her objections. Each time Meghan had calmly and logically shot down her every protest until Lucy had given in.

"As my contribution to this harebrained idea," she had started without preamble over the phone that morning, "I have a title for the thesis you're supposedly working on."

"Okay, let's have it," Meghan had said with a laugh, glad she finally had Lucy's reluctant support.

"Call it 'Ramifications of the Out-of-Town Convention Upon the Professional Male of the Species.' "

"That's great." Meghan had chuckled. "That sounds dry enough to put a real sociologist to sleep."

"Meghan"—Lucy's voice had been sober and serious—"you be careful."

"I promise I will."

Putting phase one into action, Meghan explained to the desk clerk at the Essex House Hotel that she was working on a sociology thesis and got his permission to "tactfully" conduct her survey in the lobby.

In her planning she had obtained several convention schedules from the larger hotels and had methodically eliminated possibilities until she'd come to her final decision. A Physics Symposium at the Essex. She was hoping her baby would have the intellect of a physicist and the superbly athletic body for which members of her family were known.

She had never in her wildest imagination thought it

was going to be so difficult to find one decent man to get her pregnant. She must have met hundreds of men in her life, and, of course, she'd always mentally accepted or rejected them as possible husband material. But picking out a stranger to father her baby was something else entirely.

She had, however, worked out a logical system for interviewing the candidates ambling about the lobby of the hotel. The first priority was general appearance. She didn't mind bald men, but height was a definite point of consideration. If the baby grew up to be a short person, he or she would feel inferior in the Shay family. A pot belly and thin, straight, greasy hair were probably irrelevant, but if coupled with a short stature, the conventioneer was automatically eliminated. The second factor involved was how Meghan felt about the person in general. Considering herself an excellent judge of character, she didn't approach a man unless she had a good feeling about him.

There were five hundred men attending the Physics Symposium. Of the possible subjects in the lobby, Meghan had interviewed twelve, none of whom had turned out to be the right man.

An hour later, she was in the cocktail lounge. She had explained herself to the bartender, and he had graciously given the pleasant, harmless looking sociologist free reign of his domain.

Meghan thought she had hit pay dirt when she encountered four gentlemen, whom she guessed were all in their mid-thirties, sitting at a table. They happily agreed to answer her questions, and had great fun with their responses.

"I definitely wouldn't mind taking a woman who was a total stranger, to bed," one of the men was saying, as he eyed Meghan lecherously.

Feeling extremely uncomfortable and about ready to chuck the entire project, Meghan looked away from the table, toward the entrance to the lobby.

There were people passing back and forth in front of the archway. A cluster of men were talking and shaking hands. *All these people are perfectly normal human beings*, she thought to herself. *Over half are probably married, or have been, and I'll bet most of them have fathered a child. Why can't I find just one?*

It was then she noticed him breaking away from the group. He said something to the man on his right, shook the man's hand and turned toward the lounge.

Meghan felt her breath catch in her throat. He was the most magnificent man she'd ever seen. Tall and burly, his movements were fluent and graceful. Then, as she watched him turn in response to his name and allow himself to be draped in the long white arms of Daphne Alexander, her lip curled with disgust.

Daphne traveled in the fast lane. She was one of those young, plastic society women who never seemed to have anything better to do than flirt with men and paint her toenails. Not that Meghan had anything against wealthy people in general; some of her favorite clients were well-to-do. But the idle rich who had more money than manners, more time than they knew what to do with, and who knew more gossip about their so-called friends than they knew about current world events, irritated her beyond control.

Meghan had met Daphne at several of the lavish affairs thrown by her law firm's senior partners. Meghan had always considered the events to be a bit on the garish side and found it interesting in retrospect that Daphne had always seemed right at home amid the festivities.

The giant man gave Daphne a brief, polite embrace, then stepped back as she launched into conversation. He kept nodding and smiling for several minutes, and to Meghan's delight he didn't appear to be enjoying himself very much. She almost giggled when he thrust one hand deep into his pants pocket and impatiently shifted his weight from one leg to the other. The gesture spoke volumes on his good manners.

Somewhere in the back of her mind she realized that the professor who was currently answering her last question was nearly finished. She glanced back at the men, now finding them totally lacking as specimens, and asked her next question. Their answers were irrelevant to her, but she needed time to plan her moves on "Mr. Right."

When he was finally able to break away from Daphne, he entered the lounge with an air of bold self-assurance, exuding total masculinity. Briefly scanning the room, he chose a table behind and to the left of where Meghan was sitting. Stretching out in the chair, his legs reaching under the table for what seemed like miles, he glanced up to find Meghan watching him. She saw him give her a brief half smile before she quickly drew her attention back to the four ex-candidates.

Discovering that she had been holding her breath since first seeing him, Meghan sighed.

"If I were guaranteed that my wife would never find out, I probably wouldn't hesitate very long either," another, more serious physics professor was saying.

"What?" Meghan asked, confused.

"I was answering your question," he said.

"Oh. So you would have a fling at a convention then," she restated for him.

"I would if my wife's radar were out of commission, but she's got almost a sixth sense about my faithfulness. One time I had this gorgeous blonde in one of my classes." He went on to tell his story, but Meghan's own radar was homing in on the man behind her. In her mind she reviewed the smooth contours of his face, the cap of thick, dark hair, the keenness of his eyes. . . .

Michael Ramsey was dog-tired and frustrated when he entered the cocktail lounge on the main floor of the Essex House Hotel. He'd taken the late flight out of

Dallas the night before, and since nine o'clock that morning, he'd been discussing preliminary plans to buy out a company named Dobson Publishing. It was perfect for his needs—good reputation, moderate size, excellent facilities, superb staff. But Lord, those Dobson brothers could hem and haw. They quibbled and dickered over every point as if Michael, too, were haggling . . . and he wasn't. He was very aware of what selling out meant to the two men and was more than willing to meet their demands. But after three or four hours with the picky old gentlemen, Michael's patience and understanding had begun to wear thin. He'd be glad when he could turn the whole deal over to his lawyers.

He should have gone straight up to his room, but he needed to unwind—a lot—before he would be able to sleep.

After the waitress had come and gone, leaving his drink behind, Michael looked around the lounge. Not many unattached women were out tonight, he noted absently. The majority of the people present were men in ties and suits, and an occasional woman in a business suit or casual dress. There were also several couples who were obviously out for a romantic night on the town. *Lucky them*, he thought wryly.

His attention finally settled on the group of men in front of him and the woman who had been staring at him earlier. She seemed to be throwing out topics for discussion, and the men were responding with animated conversation. She was probably a secretary, he speculated. As he watched, the woman turned her head slightly, looking from man to man, and as she did so, to Michael's bemused amazement, her hair changed colors.

As the soft lights in the darkened lounge reflected off the top of her head, her shiny red hair went from a golden copper color to chestnut, then to a flame red, and then to a deep, dark brick red. His weary, enfeebled brain found it fascinating. For several minutes he watched her in a daze.

His eyes narrowed slightly as the woman began to straighten her spine, sitting taller in her seat, her head held high. When she gave him a quick, sidelong glance, he knew she was still very aware of him.

He was amused. Women were one of his favorite sports. He tremendously enjoyed watching them use their tactics on men. He couldn't count the times a woman had set her cap for him and then proceeded to maneuver and connive to get his attentions. It was almost like a game to him to set his wits against those of the formidable fairer sex.

With the survival of his bachelorhood in mind, he sized up his latest possible opponent. Well, maybe she wasn't too much of a threat after all, he thought disappointedly. Considering the way she had quickly turned away when he had caught her looking at him, and the stylish but prim way she dressed, she was probably as shy as a church mouse. Too bad, he thought, because aside from her gorgeous hair, she also had incredible legs—beautifully shaped, and damned near as long as his.

As he examined her stems, the shy flower stood to take leave of the gentlemen. Michael's gaze followed the long, shapely limbs up to the voluptuous curves and bulges barely concealed by the conservative skirt and jacket. "Good Lord," he lamented out loud, thinking it was probably just as well that she was timid. Take down that hair, take off the glasses, and she could be a very dangerous woman.

He watched as she reluctantly turned toward him. She hesitated several seconds before she resolutely started walking toward his table. Nothing could conceal her lithe movements or the subtly seductive sway of her hips. For the first time he got a good look at her face. Her skin was creamy white, her high cheekbones flushed with a rosy glow. She had a pert, little nose that turned up slightly, and the way her chin was set at a stubbornly determined angle very much appealed to Michael.

Her eyes startled him. She looked at him straight on, and he was amazed that even through the glasses he could see how purely green they were. Her eyes were as green as her hair was red, not hazel or a mossy green, but almost a true kelly green. It fleetingly crossed his mind that she was indeed a "bonny Irish lass."

"Excuse me," she said softly. "Could I bother you by asking you a few questions?"

Michael had stood when she arrived at his table. *She couldn't be more than six inches shorter than I am,* he thought with pleasure. *At least if I kissed her, I wouldn't have to get down on my knees to do it.* The idea brought his gaze to her lips, which were soft and luscious looking. Pulling himself together as much as possible, he smiled at her.

"Certainly. What sort of questions?" he asked, offering her the chair opposite him.

"Well, it's a survey actually," she said, her voice cracking slightly. The man was magnificent. Meghan couldn't remember ever feeling so nervous or self-conscious around a man. She didn't care if he was from out of town or not at this point. If he was, he'd fit into her plan perfectly. If he was a full-blooded New Yorker . . . well, so what. Her first choice would have been to have a legal daddy for her baby, anyway; that he was big and gorgeous and sent her heart racing wouldn't hurt, either.

He looked at her with a bold honesty that made her feel as though she had "phony" written across her forehead. His face was tanned and he had little laugh lines around his eyes, eyes which were an unusual steel gray, almost teal color. Knowing instinctively that, barring venereal disease or mental illness, he was the one, she gave him extra credit for his eyes. Meghan wouldn't mind at all if her baby had his eyes and hair—it was time for a little color variation in the Shay family.

The woman was staring at him again. Poor thing. Wanting to help her, Michael prompted, "What sort of survey?"

"Oh, sorry. I'm working on a sociology thesis. There aren't very many questions; it won't take long," she recited from habit.

"Okay. Ask away. Would you like a drink?" he added, trying to make her comfortable.

"No. No, thank you." She cleared her throat gently and launched into the interview. "Your age, please?"

"Thirty-six," he stated.

Meghan was writing feverishly on the clipboard and didn't look up when she asked, "Your general health?"

"Healthy," he replied. He watched as she continued to write. "Is it taking you all that time to put down thirty-six and healthy?"

"No. Oh, no," she stammered. "I'm also writing down your general physical description."

"Why?"

He was the first man to ask her a question, and Meghan was not prepared. She suddenly became more anxious. She touched her forehead and glanced at her fingertips to see if the paint was still wet on her "phony" sign.

"I don't know," she said as frankly as she could, not understanding why herself. She wasn't likely to forget him. "Do you mind?"

"No, I don't mind, if you'll read your description to me."

Meghan had written "gorgeous hunk of man, tall, wonderful big gray eyes, long black lashes, dark wavy hair."

Truly flustered now, she responded, "I . . . I wrote tall, large frame, dark coloring, gray eyes. . . . Is that okay?"

"Will you relax? I'm not going to attack you, I promise." He chuckled at her in a friendly manner. "It's fine. Ask your next question."

"How tall are you, and what is your weight?" she went on, giving him a brief smile.

"Six-four. Two hundred and forty-five, usually," he retorted briefly. "How about you?"

"How about me what?" she asked, her green eyes round in startlement. Michael watched as even, white teeth nipped at her lower lip. It was a very inviting gesture.

"How tall are you?" he restated, his admiring gaze roving over the top half of her body.

"Five-eleven," she said, watching him look at her, increasingly aware of her own femininity. Her heart rate accelerated and her flushed cheeks began to burn with a sensation she hesitated to identify.

However, his glance was not a leer, she noted. It was merely admiring. His eyes were friendly, and he had intended the look to be a compliment, not a lecherous advance.

Nervously, she cleared her throat once more and spoke before he could ask her anything else.

"Do you have a family or personal history of diabetes?"

"No."

"Allergies?"

"No."

"Mental illness?"

"Mental illness?" he repeated.

Meghan nodded, giving him the innocent look that had always worked on her father, except when she'd been caught red-handed.

"No," he stated with a perplexed frown, as he motioned for the waitress to bring him another drink. "Are you sure you won't join me?"

"No, thank you. Do you happen to know your I.Q.?" she asked, beginning to feel a little more at ease with him. He was really a very nice man; she could feel it in her bones.

"No, I don't. Sorry," he apologized.

"That's okay," she said casually, before asking, "Do you take illegal drugs?"

He eyed her suspiciously now. "Does that have something to do with my IQ?"

"I'm not sure. I suppose it could, but it's just one of the questions," she informed him with a shrug.

"No, I don't take illegal drugs," he answered, still frowning. He was about to take a sip of scotch from his glass when she dropped her first bomb.

"Do you have a social disease?"

Michael coughed and sputtered after having gasped and inhaled part of his drink. A worried Meghan was instantly at his side, giving his back several well-intended blows. Gulping air to return the oxygen to his brain so he could think again, he scrutinized her with sharp eyes.

"Did I hear you correctly?" he asked, dumbfounded, pushing his drink to the side of the table.

"It is one of the questions, but if you'd rather not answer . . ." Her best attorney's voice was interrupted.

"Hell, no, I don't have a social disease," he almost yelled at her. "What . . ."

This time she interrupted him before she lost her nerve.

"Would you happen to know whether or not you're sterile?" she threw at him, putting on a totally guileless expression.

"Who are you?" he asked, stunned and a little angry.

"Well, these questionnaires are usually totally anonymous. I don't think that they include my name either. I'm just someone asking someone else a question." She squirmed in her chair, hoping he'd find his sense of humor soon, before she had to cross him off the top of her list.

For several minutes he just sat still, his head cocked to one side, considering her. As the silence became uncomfortable, Meghan became flustered again. It wasn't going right. She didn't want to offend him, but there were certain things she needed to know. Trying to calm herself, she attempted a new approach.

"Look, mister, this is just a survey for a sociology thesis. I don't want to pry into your life or offend you. Let's just call it quits," she bluffed, starting to rise from her chair.

He reached out and put a hand on her clipboard. "Sit . . . please," he said, his thick Texas drawl gentle. "You are prying into my life, but in answer to your question, to my knowledge, it's yet to be confirmed."

The woman was a Chinese puzzle to Michael. How could she look like a wallflower one minute, and then without batting an eye, ask him intimate questions the next. Maybe he'd misjudged her. Maybe she was just extremely wily. He began to visualize how she'd look without the glasses, with her hair down. . . .

"Would you describe your education," she requested, breaking into his reverie.

"I have degrees in American Literature and Journalism, and an MBA," he rattled off, his mind on far more interesting things.

"And you teach physics?" Meghan asked, frowning in confusion.

He thought he must have missed part of the conversation. "I don't teach physics," he said simply.

"What do you mean, you don't teach physics?" she questioned, panic rising in her voice.

"I mean, I don't teach physics. I'm a publisher," he clarified. As she sat gawking at him as though he had suddenly grown horns on his head, he tried to be helpful. "You know—books, magazines, newspapers."

"Where?" she uttered.

"Where what?"

"Where do you publish?" she asked testily.

"Texas and California at the moment."

She sighed audibly, visibly calmed by his answer.

"So you don't live in New York?" she said, wanting it made perfectly clear.

"I live in Dallas," he said thoughtfully, then added, "You know, this is the strangest survey I've ever heard . . . or answered. What's this thesis about, anyway?"

"The Ramification of the Out-of-Town Convention Upon the Professional Male of the Species," she said, grinning at him.

A deep chuckle rose from inside him. His eyes twinkled as he shared her enjoyment of the title.

"That sounds dry enough to put any sociologist to sleep," he observed in his deep, fatigue-slurred voice.

Meghan laughed aloud as he nearly quoted her remark to Lucy that morning. "I didn't dream up the title," she confessed honestly, "I'm just asking the questions."

"Well, I answered your questions, but I'm not attending a convention," he pointed out to her.

She looked around, doing an excellent impression of a CIA agent, then leaned forward and curled her index finger at him. He looked from side to side, joining in the game, and came face to face with her across the table. His breath was warm on her face. They grinned at one another, their gazes locked. In the few seconds before Meghan spoke, they seemed to have exchanged something with their eyes. A secret? A promise? A sensation? A bond of some kind? She didn't know what it was, but she knew they both were aware of it. She knew that if they parted in the next minute, they each would remember having shared *something* indefinable for a few brief seconds in the dim lounge of the Essex House Hotel.

"You know that. And now I know it," she whispered. "But do you think anyone reading the thesis will?"

"Nope." His grin widened. The amused twinkle in his eyes was intoxicating. Meghan willingly could have drowned in them. Why couldn't he live in New York after all, she thought. She could forget this whole thing and do it the right way . . . with him.

"To tell you the truth," she continued to whisper conspiratorily, "asking these questions of strange men is terribly embarrassing and not a lot of fun for me. So if you don't mind being mixed in with a few physics professors, I'm just going to shuffle your answers in with theirs and call it a night."

"You mean you've finished?" he asked, his brows raising with interest.

"Yes. Thank heavens," she said, leaning back in her chair again, oddly breathless.

"Will you join me for a drink then?" he asked, also returning to a relaxed position, aware that he was hoping very hard she would stay. Sometime during the last few minutes she had lost that shy, uncertain air. Her eyes had taken on a look of self-assuredness, and she was smiling in a shrewd, knowing manner. Michael was intrigued.

"Again, thank you, but I really can't." She paused briefly and gave him a very special smile. "I do thank you for answering those awkward questions though," she said as she gathered her things and prepared to leave. The last question on her list that she had not asked was whether or not, as a conventioneer, he would have a brief fling if the opportunity arose. It was a superfluous question at this point. She already knew that she was going to do all in her power to have him.

"Are you a sociologist then?" Michael asked, ignoring her readiness to leave, wanting to know more about her.

"No," she admitted, "but I'm in a related field, and the subject of the individual human being in society has always interested me," and felt good at being truthful with him.

"You enjoy your work. That's good. So many people don't," he said, for no real purpose other than to keep her talking about herself.

Meghan studied him thoughtfully. He looked tired. Lines of fatigue etched his face, and his eyelids drooped over blood-shot eyes, even as said orbs danced with friendliness and interest.

"Life is too short to do something you don't like, just as it's too short not to fill it with all the things you want to do, or have, or be," she said sincerely.

"I agree," Michael solidly confirmed. His eyes narrowed slightly as he sat across from her, each of them measuring, speculating, forming opinions of the other. So what if she didn't dress to do her beauty justice; she was thoughtful and intelligent . . . and not at all shy, he determined as he watched her boldly assess his own features. This woman was different. She didn't seem to be at all aware of her good looks, or if she was, it didn't matter to her. She gave the impression of someone who enjoyed living and fulfilling her life to her own satisfaction, as opposed to someone who simply floated through her existence, dreaming but never achieving. This woman achieved.

"You're not a native New Yorker," he stated more than questioned.

"No," she said, and grinned. "I developed my twang in Boston, but I've lived in New York for so long, people hardly notice it anymore. Strange the way people adapt to their surroundings," she speculated. "Even their voices change. However, I do think that drawl of yours would be very hard to alter, even after living in New York," she added with a warm-hearted laugh.

"Again, I agree with you," he said with a nod of his head and a good-natured laugh. "But then, we Texans tend to hold on to things once we got 'em," Michael informed Meghan in a thicker-than-thick stage drawl.

"Well, that's good, because I like it," she confessed, still smiling happily as she made her move to leave him. "I really have to go, but thanks again for being such a good sport about the questionnaire. I enjoyed talking with you," she said, holding out her hand in a friendly gesture.

Neither was prepared for the small flash of sparks that flew when Michael took Meghan's hand. Their arms tingled in the aftermath of the shock; their eyes registered their wonderment. They were silent for several seconds.

"There's no way I could talk you into staying a little longer?" he asked hopefully.

Meghan gave a regretful shrug. "I'm sorry. But maybe we'll run into each other again sometime." It was more of a promise than a prophecy.

"I'd like that. And I wish you luck on your project," Michael said, knowing he'd kick himself later for letting her get away.

"Thank you," she replied sincerely, standing to leave. "It will make me very happy if it turns out the way I'm hoping it will."

A short time later the waitress approached Michael.

"Would you like another?" she asked politely, cataloging his good looks with interest.

He considered having another drink. He felt restless, disconcerted, and strangely exasperated. It was that woman, that redhead. He didn't even know her name. The Red-Headed Woman With No Name. It sounded like the title of a B movie. He kept picturing her walking toward him with that alluring sway of her hips. In the next sequence, her glasses were gone, and her glorious red hair hung in waves to the middle of her back. Subsequently, she sauntered toward him in nothing but a black teddy. At this point his heart would race and he'd feel definite signs of quickening in his body. Then the film would begin again in his mind.

He glanced up and realized the waitress was waiting for his answer. Maybe another drink would destroy the haunting memory. . . . Then again, he was so tired and

the two drinks he'd already had had relaxed him considerably. If he drank any more, the Red-Headed Woman
would come riding in on a pink elephant.

"No. Thanks. I'll just finish this one," he said morosely.

In the ladies' room just outside the cocktail lounge,
Meghan had removed her glasses and jacket, changed
shoes and was unbraiding her hair in front of the large
mirror.

Second, third, and fourth thoughts of carrying out
her self-imposed assignment riddled her conscience.
The man was perfect. Wonderful genes. A stranger from
out of town. He fit the bill exactly. Going to bed with
him wouldn't be too painful, either, Meghan thought
wryly. As a bonus, he was dead on his feet with exhaustion. He would probably pass out immediately afterward and there wouldn't be any uncomfortable scenes.

"Have you thought about a man's right to know about
his own children?" came Lucy's voice, honest and frank.

"Damn," Meghan said aloud, pulling a brush from
her bag and dragging it through her tight waves of
hair.

A sleazy character had been out of the question from
the beginning. She had pictured a decent looking, ego-
tistical but essentially harmless womanizer. A faceless,
walking, talking spermmobile of sorts. But this nice,
honorable man?

He had probably never slain a dragon or settled a
violent labor dispute single-handedly. He may never
have been an Eagle Scout or given a quarter to a stranger
for a phone call, but Meghan felt he wouldn't hesitate
to do so. He had integrity. It showed in his face and the
way he carried himself. He was a good man. Wasn't he?

Guilt and uncertainty warred with her own wants
and needs and rights. Childishly, she pouted that it
didn't seem fair that the man played such a large part
in the creation of a baby when it was the woman who

did all the work. She fortified herself, thinking that one little spark in a man's eye could bloat a woman's body, cause her the untold pain of delivery, and give her a lifetime of moral, physical, mental, and emotional responsibilities.

Calmly, she asked herself, "Do you really want a baby?" "Yes," she answered. "So when will a more perfect subject come along again?" Meghan could tell her muse was all for going ahead with the plan. And she was right. The chances of the right man and the right time coming together again at a convenient place were almost nil.

In two and a half hours or less she'd be home and in her own bed. He'd wake up in the morning, get on a plane, and never look back. He'd never even know what hit him. She had no intentions of hurting the man in any way. What he didn't know, couldn't hurt him. But what she didn't know about him, could hurt her, came her hundredth thought. Under normal circumstances, she'd trust her first instincts about a person without question. But this was far from a normal situation even for Meghan on one of her more outlandish days, of which there had been several in years gone by. Was she so desperate to have a baby that she'd delude herself into going to bed with a gorgeous murderer? Could she trust her nearly faultless instincts in a case such as this?

Loath though she was to admit it, there was a way for her to be certain. Daphne Alexander. Meghan rolled her eyes in dread and dismay. It was better to be safe than sorry.

Finishing her transformation, she hurriedly found a quarter. For authenticity and to avert suspicion, she used the pay phone rather than the house phone to call the main desk.

She chewed on her lower lip anxiously while she prayed Daphne was still in the Essex and able to hear the page.

"Hello," rang Daphne's sugar-sweet voice over the line moments later.

"Ms. Alexander," Meghan started enthusiastically, "This is Meghan Shay. I understand you called."

"I did?" Daphne asked, her tone vague.

"That's the message I got from my secretary," she said simply, inferring her secretary had better things to do than make up false messages.

"Well, I did call once, at your office," the society darling admitted, still confused, "but that was about two months ago."

"How may I help you?" Meghan said, as if a two month waiting period were customary, glad she hadn't returned Daphne's call earlier. It was strange the way things always had a way of working themselves out, Meghan decided philosophically.

"How did you know where to reach me at this time of night?" the not-so-stupid debutante asked.

"Ah . . ." Meghan had to think quick. "I was on my way out of the Essex a little while ago and saw you. I knew you wouldn't have called me at the office unless it was important, so when I got home, I thought I'd try to reach you there. Have I interrupted something?" she asked politely, humoring the girl.

"Actually, I, . . ." Daphne paused. Apparently deciding the information she'd wanted two months ago was still important enough to preempt whatever she was doing at the moment, she continued, "I called to see if you'd enjoyed the party at the Clarensons'. They're such lovely people and always make their guests feel so comfortable."

"Yes, they are," agreed Meghan, frowning disjointedly. "I had a lovely time."

"I suppose that handsome young man you were with had something to do with that as well," Daphne mentioned none too discreetly.

A sly, knowing smile curved Meghan's lips. "Tim?

Oh, yes, he's a doll. A really nice person," she said with enthusiasm.

"Have you known him long?" Daphne asked.

"No, not really, but I wish I had time to get to know him better. I'm just so busy, I never seem to find time for dating. And men like Tim don't come along every day," Meghan responded with just the right amount of wistfulness. "I saw for myself that that isn't the case for you though. I saw you hugging that enormous man in the lobby of the Essex a little while ago. He was nothing to spit at," Meghan said teasingly, but in fact she was very truthful.

"Oh, him. You're right. He isn't anything to ignore, but he's very picky. He's nice, don't get me wrong, but he doesn't . . . play around much, if you know what I mean. He likes to joke around, but he's real serious about his publishing company and keeps his private life . . . private."

"He's antisocial?" concluded Meghan, her mind suspicious.

"Not at all," rushed Daphne, unaware that her brain was being picked almost clean. "It's just that he doesn't run with our crowd even though he's been invited often enough. When he's not behind his desk, he's into horses and cows and sports and staying healthy. Things like that," she explained, as if "things like that" were terribly low class interests. "But basically, he's a really nice guy."

The self-satisfied grin and devilish glint in Meghan's eyes would have terrified the calmest soul. "He certainly was handsome," she reiterated.

"Oh, yes, he is that, but so was that Tim you were with at the Clarensons'. What was his last name again? I've forgotten." Daphne was nothing if not obvious.

Tim Brogan wasn't a particularly close friend of Meghan's; she hardly knew him. How would she know whether Daphne wasn't just exactly the type of woman he was looking for? It wouldn't be like feeding him to the wolves; he could always say no for himself.

"Brogan," Meghan stated quickly, before she changed her mind. After all, she sort of owed Daphne one. "Tim Brogan. He's in real estate development and making a killing at it, from all accounts."

"How interesting," Daphne cooed. Meghan could almost see the saliva dripping from Daphne's fangs and suddenly felt sorry for poor Tim.

"Thank you for calling, Daphne. I've enjoyed talking to you, but I have to run," Meghan said, unable to resist the temptation to scatter Daphne's thoughts once more.

"It was my pleasure, Meghan. We'll talk again soon," replied Daphne, none the worse for wear.

Meghan could only shake her head disbelievingly as she hung up the phone. Then she settled her attention firmly on the task at hand. Reassured that her good judgment was intact, she set out to complete phase one.

Two

Michael was nearly finished with his drink, which was now more melted ice than scotch. Why he was still sitting there sipping warm scotch-flavored water, he didn't know. He was so tired that he was contemplating taking a cab up to his room. At least the movie was over. He heaved a long sigh of relief.

Or was it? There she was again, coming from the direction of the lobby this time. Whoa! The film had been tampered with. It was her vamp scene—hair down, no glasses, sexy clothes, the seductive sway in excellent form.

His lips parted in a silent gasp. He took in her every nuance as she came to a standstill at his elbow. So beautiful, so real looking.

"Is that offer for a drink still good?" she asked in a low, soft, sultry voice.

He could only nod dumbly. She circled behind him and took the seat near his left arm. She gracefully crossed her long legs, her skirt rising up temptingly. There was a small inviting smile on her lips and an age-old glint in her eyes.

Somewhere in the back of his mind he knew he'd fallen asleep in a cocktail lounge, but all he could do was pray that the barmaid didn't wake him up.

Michael had heard of sexual fantasies such as this. Dreams that seemed so real, you woke up sweating and breathless and exhausted. He wasn't complaining. This one had far more electricity and excitement in it than the one he had as a teenager, in which a half-naked woman rode across his grandfather's range on an Appaloosa horse. He supposed it was his turn to say something. Without a script, he improvised with the first thing that came to mind.

"You . . . are . . . stunning," he said, his drawl thick, his gaze caressing every inch of her.

"As are you," she said softly, sincerely.

"No more questions?" he asked.

"You know what they say about all work and no play making Jill a dull girl," she returned, intimating that it was definitely time to play.

"Your name's Jill?" He seized the information hopefully.

"Jill will do if you need a name." She smiled and watched him through the thick fringe of her lashes.

"Jill," he repeated, rolling the name around in his mouth. New subtitle: The Red-Headed Woman Named Jill. "I like it," he said aloud, too tired and stunned to question her response.

"You don't look well. Are you going to be able to get to your room?" she asked solicitously, knowing the time was now or never. He would slip into a coma, or she would lose her nerve soon. If she was going to get impregnated, she needed to get things rolling.

She had never seen a man look so devastatingly handsome and virile and so vulnerable at the same time. Spending one night with him would be like taking candy from a baby—and she loved babies.

Michael's thoughts were on a parallel course to the same destination. He was enjoying the smooth cleverness of his sophisticated fantasy. The playwright was very good.

"Actually, I was thinking of calling a cab," he said truthfully. "But if I could impose on your kindness for a little help, I could probably use some of the fresh air between here and the elevators."

"It's no imposition. Besides, I owe you one for answering all those ridiculous questions."

Skillful, yet subtle. Michael mentally applauded her.

And this is how I'm going to repay him, Meghan thought, her reserve faltering for a second.

"Are you ready?" she asked, as he just slouched there gazing at her, naked desire in his eyes.

"What about your drink?" he asked.

Glad he wasn't completely in a stupor, Meghan flashed him a breathtaking smile. She promised herself that if he stayed awake long enough to service her, he wouldn't regret it. In return, she would give him all the pleasure she possibly could. The idea was titillating. This mammoth man was physically very exciting. Her fingers were itching to touch him. Meghan guessed he would be as hard as a rock, as strong as a bear, and as warm as the Texas sun. The squirming knot low in her abdomen and the ticklish, tingling sensations running up and down her body as he studied each facet of her was, she knew, her own nervousness in this situation.

"Some other time," she told him, dismissing the drink and standing.

He rose slowly to his full, towering height. He didn't move for several seconds as his head adjusted to the altitude. Then he turned and motioned for her to precede him. As she came alongside him, he placed a big, warm hand flat on the small of her naked back.

Once again, they were both shocked—she from the sparks that warmed her skin and tripped her heartbeat into overdrive, he from the fact that she was not only braless and shirtless from behind, but that she was also very warm and soft for a mirage.

He made a mental note to instruct his secretary to book all his future visits to New York at the Essex— they served great scotch.

The trip to his room was uneventful. Michael didn't

take his eyes off her for fear that she'd disappear and he'd find he really was walking down the hallway alone.

He unlocked the door to his suite and stood aside for her to enter. She hesitated briefly, then walked into the room. He put the key on the table in the foyer and followed her into the sitting room. He shrugged out of his jacket and laid it over the back of a chair. Loosening his tie, he turned to her. Incredibly beautiful and provocative, she stood tall and confident in the center of the room.

Neither Michael nor his apparition had spoken since they'd left the lounge, but the air was thick with messages. Somewhere along the way, Michael had taken on the uneasy feeling that this was not the dream he thought it was. Oh, she was enchanting, for sure, and he hadn't imagined the seduction in her eyes, either. But Michael was not an idiot, nor was he out of his mind with fatigue. Tired and suffering from jet lag, yes, but not yet unconscious. Something was definitely happening here.

"May I order up some coffee for you? Or maybe your drink?" he asked politely.

She shook her head slightly, her gaze never leaving his face as he studied her.

His desire for her was not a delusion either. She had the kind of body a man wouldn't tire of quickly—and he was only human. But every woman he'd ever known had a motive behind her actions. Some were motivated by love, some by money or other favors, some were just manipulative. It was true he'd taken women to bed out of pure mutual lust, but he'd also known them longer than an hour and a half. So what motive drove The Red-Headed Woman Named Jill?

He moved over to the couch and sat down, turning slightly to indicate that he expected her to follow his lead and sit next to him.

"Maybe we'll just talk awhile," he suggested in a deep, husky baritone voice.

This time, as she gave the red cloud around her face a short negative shake, she reached both of her hands behind her. He heard the soft whiz of a zipper being pulled before her hands returned to her sides and her skirt slipped from her hips to pool at her feet.

Every nerve in Michael's body stood on end, his heart raced, and he recognized the familiar throbbing between his legs as he ravished her with his eyes. She was spectacular. A perfect contrast of colors—black on white. The black stockings accentuated the soft curves of her long, lean legs and the lace of the garter belt displayed the smooth, creamy perfection of her skin.

Slowly, her hands went behind her again. The lower bands of the backless blouse fell forward wickedly. It wasn't until she had reached up behind her neck to loosen the rest of the garment, her hardened nipples pressing against the silky material, that Michael was finally jolted into action.

He sprang from the couch with a grace and speed Meghan hadn't expected in someone his size. He grabbed her savagely by the forearms and slammed her up against his hard body. Meghan's head fell back and she looked up into his ferocious face, his eyes a cold steel gray with anger.

"You stupid little fool," he said through clenched teeth. "How do you know I wasn't lying downstairs? How do you know insanity doesn't run wild in my family? How do you know I won't take all you're offering and then break your lovely little neck?"

The panic that rose up in Meghan was earthshaking, but growing up in an Irish family full of poker players had proven useful more than once. As he raged at her, thoughts raced through her mind. Did Daphne know her head from a hole in the wall? Surely she must! *He's a good, decent man. I know he is. He's honorable and trustworthy. I feel it.* Besides, a lunatic wouldn't warn someone of his intentions. Or would he? No. No, he wouldn't. Not when she was making it so easy for him.

Ah, that was it! Meghan's very logical mind grasped at a calming chord. *He is a decent, honorable man—and that's why he's warning me.* As her mind became as tranquil as her expression, her heart went out to the man who'd won her respect and admiration.

"I've always been an excellent judge of character," she told him softly and honestly.

His eyes narrowed as he looked deeply into hers, trying to fathom her thoughts. Hers weren't crazy or sinister eyes. They were full of trust and warmth and longing. He had hoped his violent act would scare her, but she never once showed any fear. She was obviously a mature woman in control of herself. And she obviously wanted him.

Michael knew he sure as hell wanted her. He could smell the lavender scent she wore. She was warm and soft, and her body seemed to melt into the contours of his. She was an incredible creature.

To Meghan's delight, his facial features softened as his morals and suspicions gave way to his overcharged libido.

He released his grip on her arms and placed her palms on his chest. Skillful hands slid up to her shoulders, leaving tingling gooseflesh in their wake. Their gazes never wavered as he moved to release the clasp at her neck. The blouse slid down to the tops of her breasts and stopped where their bodies met. His hands remained at the nape of her neck, his thumbs sliding around her ears to gently caress the hollows of her cheeks.

He lowered his head to rest his lips on hers in a tender, tentative kiss. Her full lips were soft and warm and pliable. Michael felt a sudden surge of adrenaline shoot through his body. He raised his head. Frowning in wonderment, he studied her once again. Had she felt it too? Something magical happened every time he touched her. Was she as affected as he was?

Apparently she was, he thought with amused pleasure. She had snaked her arms around his neck and was pulling his head forward to meet her lips with his.

They explored each other's lips slowly, gently, teasingly at first. Michael's tongue parted her lips to taste the sensitive tissues inside. Meghan opened her mouth eagerly for him, and their kiss deepened.

Breathless and trembling, they pulled apart slightly, the surprise of their discovery evident in their eyes. Michael's hands now rested on her hips, where he played with the lacy garter belt. He pulled himself from her a little more, but didn't release her. Her cleverly seductive blouse fell to the floor at last.

He took a step backward to see her better, and Meghan let him drink in his fill. He did so with an unabashed thirst. Her coloring fascinated him. The creaminess of her skin, flushed rosy with excitement, was especially pleasing to him. He grazed the top of one breast with his hand.

"You have so few freckles for a redhead. You must be very careful in the sun," he commented absently.

"Just lucky," she murmured, wallowing in the sensations he created as he touched a pink, hard-tipped nipple with his thumb.

"You're incredibly beautiful," he said in a low, husky voice.

He kissed her deeply, his hands moving restlessly over her nakedness. She pressed her body into his, as if she couldn't get close enough to him. Meghan's head began to spin. She could feel herself trembling as her knees turned to jelly.

It startled her when he swept her effortlessly off her feet and into his arms, cradling her close to his chest.

She giggled.

"You'll break your back," she cautioned him. "I'm no munchkin, you know."

"I did notice that," he said solemnly, an amused twinkle warming his eyes. "And if I were planning a fifty-mile trek through a jungle to civilization, you'd have to do your own walking. As it is," he said, lowering her feet gently to the floor beside his bed, "twenty feet to the nearest bed was not too much to handle—it was even enjoyable."

"And very romantic," she said, grinning as her fingers finished loosening the knot in his tie.

"Are you a romantic?" he asked, realizing again how little he knew about the beautiful woman. Aside from her luscious body and the fact that she might not have any wire in her bailing machine, he knew nothing.

"Sometimes," she answered thoughtfully.

"But not always."

"No. Not always," she said wistfully, as she started to unbutton his shirt. When the opening was wide enough, she slipped her hands inside and ran her fingers through the lush crop of crisp, black hair.

"Mmm," she sighed, relishing the feel of him. The hard muscles of his chest quivered under her touch.

He moved around to sit on the bed, turning her with him. He reached out and released one garter, then slid his hand between her legs to release the other. His touch was gentle yet searing, sending wave after wave of burning currents through Meghan's body, only to be captured and rekindled deep in the core of her womanhood.

He used a soft pressure on the back of her leg to draw her right foot up to rest on his knee. Erotically, he slid his fingers down her leg, removing the stocking as he went. He concentrated on his efforts, memorizing every inch he exposed. While he repeated the ceremony on her left leg, Meghan slipped the catches on the belt and it fell away from her.

There was no amusement in his eyes when he finished and looked up to see her clad only in black string bikini panties. As he stood, he trailed his hands up the entire outside length of her legs until he reached her waist. Their gazes locked hypnotically, both seeing their own desire in the other's eyes.

Leisurely, he proceeded to undress himself for Meghan. Always a little self-conscious about letting men see her naked, Meghan was vaguely aware of how natural it seemed, how comfortable she felt, letting this man look at her and examining him in return. *Maybe it's because he's a stranger*, she thought, although for some odd reason, he didn't seem like one. She felt as if everything she'd done or would do tonight was meant to be, as if it had been preordained at her birth that this night would come to be.

The man was unique. He was powerful, yet infinitely gentle; honorable and righteous, but human and vulnerable. She enjoyed looking at him, she thrilled at his touch, she felt . . . like someone else. No man had ever affected her this way, she had never wanted a man like she wanted him—and she didn't even know his name.

It didn't matter. Their passion buffered them from the outside world. Alone, they made their own rules as only two nameless human beings strongly attracted to each other could.

He stood naked before her, his manhood proud and erect, his skin smooth over finely toned muscles. He came to her and eased her back on the bed. Kneeling over her for several seconds, he let his gaze rove slowly up her body until he reached her eyes.

His kisses were deep and sensual as his hands relished the feel of her, finding her most sensitive spots. Then he lowered his head to deliver little sipping kisses to those places. Meghan's mind and body were frantic with excitement. She writhed and twisted seductively under him. She kissed and gently nibbled as much of him as she could reach, frustrated at only being able to get to his face, neck, shoulders and arms.

Gradually, she rolled him off her and onto his back. She straddled his hips with her legs and proceeded to pleasure him in every way she knew and in some ways she'd only read about. The rumbling in his chest was like that of a large, fierce cat purring with contentment.

When his hands rose to return the pleasure, Meghan pinned them loosely above his head. With her face close to his, she looked into eyes flaming with passion.

"Please," she whispered, her lips brushing his. "Please, just let me give this to you."

"If you give me any more, I'll explode. Besides, I can't remember enjoying the feel of a woman more than I do you. Your skin is incredibly soft," he said, his voice strained.

She teased him with an erotic wiggle, causing their damp bodies to tense with the need for release. His breathing was rapid and ragged, and he quivered at her every touch. Meghan found his responses rather heady. She enjoyed delighting him and could tell he was pleased with her.

She allowed him partial entry to her ultimate softness, playfully testing the feel of his swollen masculinity with her muscles. The look of surprise he flashed at her vanished rapidly, replaced by a look full of pure deviltry.

Taking her firmly in his arms, he flipped her onto her back and grinned down at her menacingly.

"You beautiful little witch," he said, then thrust himself home, filling her completely. "Two can play that game."

"You didn't like it?" she asked innocently, knowing he had. Then she grinned at him daringly.

"You know I did. But you were enjoying yourself too much at my benefit." He chuckled dangerously. "Now we'll see if you can take it as well as you dish it out."

Very deliberately, he aroused her to a state of wild excitement, teasing and tempting until she was frantic. He took mercy on her only when he could no longer control himself. He thrust deeply, sending them both into oblivion.

He held her close as she trembled in the aftermath, as his own tremors of desire slowly subsided. Their breathing gradually regulated itself, and their heart beats slowed to normal as their satiated bodies relaxed.

Leaving her, he slid to one side, but kept her close in his arms.

"Are you all right, darlin'?" he murmured, placing a tender kiss on her temple.

She nodded, too spent to speak.

He pressed another kiss to the corner of her eye and was surprised to taste the salty wetness of her tears. Up on one elbow instantly, he looked into the limpid pools of green.

"Did I hurt you?" he asked, deeply concerned.

She shook her head as the tears fell more freely.

"What's wrong, darlin'? Can you tell me?" His deep voice rumbled solicitously.

"I . . . I think you're the . . . the most wonderful man I've ever met," Meghan told him sincerely.

He bussed her on the nose and grinned.

"Well, with you being such an excellent judge of character, you're probably right. But it's definitely not worth crying about," he said, lying down again and throwing his leg over hers. "Once you really get to know me, you'll have to think of a better word than just wonderful." He chuckled deep in his chest.

Meghan's heart soared at the pleasing sound. She could listen to his deep voice and his good-natured laughter forever. She could stay warm and safe in his arms for the rest of time. Why couldn't things be different for them? she asked herself, her soul melancholy. Then she recalled her original purpose for being there. Her baby. Somewhere along the way she had totally forgotten about the baby. The man had completely consumed her every thought. She had been concentrating only on making love to this gentle giant. Making love? No. What they'd shared had been fantastic sex. People didn't fall in love in an hour. He would go back to Texas, and she would go on with her life. He'd forget her, and she would remember this as the night she tried to get pregnant by a wonderful man.

"What's your earliest childhood memory?" he asked drowsily. "How old were you?"

"Ah . . . the first really clear memory I have is of my first day of school. I was six. The others are a little fuzzy. Why?" she asked with a confused frown, wondering what her memories had to do with the moment.

"You can start there," he murmured, cuddling closer. "I want to know all about you."

"Hmm . . ." Meghan hummed thoughtfully. He'd be asleep soon. What harm was there in telling him a bedtime story? She wanted him to know her; she wanted to know him. If only things could have been different. . . . "I went to a private school, so it was my first experience wearing a uniform. The nuns lined us up in the school yard according to our grade levels. I remember my brother leaving me in line and going off to join his own class. I was so scared. Then a huge dog came bouncing across the playground, right at me," she said, recalling her fear. "I dropped my brown lunch sack and started to scream. The dog ran up and snatched my lunch bag and then ran off. I cried for my brother, but his class had already gone in. It was a terrible morning, but the next thing I remember is eating lunch with my brother. We shared his . . ." There was a gentle snore in Meghan's right ear. "After school I roamed the streets of Boston with my father's shotgun, looking for that dog. When I found him, I demanded that he return my lunch or pay the price. . . ."

Michael had fallen asleep. Meghan waited for his breathing to deepen, and when she knew he was in a sound sleep, she slowly, carefully slipped out of his embrace. Coming around to his side of the bed to retrieve her underwear, she watched him for several seconds. Impulsively, she bent to kiss his forehead. His long, black lashes fanned out over his cheekbones endearingly. She lightly touched his rumpled hair, kissed him again, and whispered, "Thank you."

Three

Late October in New York was dreary, rainy, and cold. However, the trees in Central Park were changing colors, and there was a crispness in the air that Meghan associated with the happy Halloweens of her childhood. She always made several trips to the Park in the fall just to view the magnificent foliage. On display were her colors—the greens, yellows, browns, and reds. This was her season. The whole world changed to compliment her. She walked along the footpath, shuffling her feet through the leaves that had fallen to the ground.

Ambiguity was the emotion of the month. Not toward the baby, of course, but toward herself. She recalled the night of the baby's conception. She'd lain awake for hours, wondering if she'd be able to move on to phase two. Wondering about the man who could be the father of her child. Every time she thought of him, she was flooded with a feeling of regret. Why couldn't he have been a New Yorker? Why couldn't they have met under more normal circumstances?

When Lucy had called early the next day to check on her, Meghan told her the entire story.

"You know," Meghan confided, "it all made *so* much sense. It still does, but I . . . I don't know. I . . . I feel sort of guilty for some reason."

"Maybe you're feeling a little like a cheap pickup," Lucy offered helpfully, a teasing tone in her voice.

"Well, I definitely couldn't look the man straight in the eye again," she admitted. "But it's more than just that. I feel like a thief. Like I stole something from him."

"Don't worry about it, Meghan. What's done is done. You'll never see the man again, and it's highly unlikely that he'd take you to court over a mere four hundred million missing sperm," Lucy assured her, still amused.

"For a doctor, you make up the sickest jokes I've ever heard, Lucy," Meghan quipped, ending their conversation.

It seemed as though she'd known Lucy forever, but in actuality it had been only ten years. They had been freshmen at Harvard together. Two more unlikely people to become such close friends never existed. They were complete and total opposites.

Lucy's parents had paid her way through college and then medical school. Meghan had earned scholarships, taken out loans, and worked her way through till she graduated from law school. Lucy was blond, blue eyed, and petite. Meghan was red haired, green eyed, and tall. Lucy chose to join a group of doctors who managed a "pay as you may" prenatal and obstetrics clinic in Hoboken because she "wasn't in medicine for the money." She'd married a truly nice antique dealer and had given birth to a son who was now two-and-a-half years old. Meghan, on the other hand, had become a clever but equitable corporate attorney with the distinguished firm of Alderman, Darkwell & Gibbs. Financial security was one of her prime objectives, taking second place only to her desire to have her own family someday.

Both women were true to their parentage. Lucy vacillated from benign optimism to fatalistic doom, depending on the situation, while Meghan, sharp-witted and hot-tempered, doggedly held to her initial reactions. Except in this case.

She felt innocent of any wrongdoing to the man, but

guilty too. She hoped he never set foot in New York again, but she wanted to see him. Her greatest desire was to be pregnant, but she'd never repeat that night.

Two weeks later when the twenty-eight day cycle she'd been able to schedule vacations by didn't come to an end, she knew her fate was sealed. There was no turning back. By then her guilt had manifested itself. It was moral guilt. If her pregnancy had been an accident, she could have been guileless in her joy. As it was, her calculated intent marred her enthusiasm and heavied her heart with shame.

Now she was over three and a half months into her pregnancy, and for short periods of time she could still put the whole incident out of her mind. Aside from the tenderness in her breasts, occasional short bouts of nausea, constant fatigue, and rare episodes of dizziness if she got up too fast, there was no evidence to tell anyone, including herself, that she was going to have a baby.

She was handling the situation at the office very well, she thought self-indulgently. Although her blouses were a little tighter than usual, it wasn't noticeable to the uninformed eye. Her business outfits still fit perfectly over her slim hips and essentially flat abdomen. Thank God for physical fitness!

Her secretary, Greta, had cast a peculiar look at her when she'd found the box of saltine crackers in her desk drawer. So Meghan had covered up her symptoms of nausea by explaining that the crackers were just a low-calorie snack for late-afternoon attacks of the munchies.

When she'd lunged for Henry Alderman's desk to keep herself upright during a dizzy spell, she had confided to him about the anemia Lucy was treating her for. That excuse had worked well to explain her pallor and fatigue, and headed her list of reasons for a year-long leave of absence from the firm.

"Are you sure it's going to take that long to get back

on your feet?" Henry Alderman had asked, none too pleased with her request. "Couldn't you just take six months or so and come back to a lighter load?"

"Actually, that's my plan, Henry. I thought I'd take six months to recoup and build up my strength, and then maybe do some *pro bono* work down at Legal Aid for a few months. Just a few cases, you know, to freshen up my skills and mind. A change of pace, so that when I come back, I'll be ready and more than eager to get back to corporate law again."

"When's all this supposed to happen?"

"Well, I wanted to give you plenty of notice. Enough time to break in a couple of extra paralegals. I thought maybe mid-December. The holidays are generally a slow time. Business doesn't usually pick up again until February. By then you'll have forgotten all about me, except for my name on the door," she had said, grinning at him infectiously.

"Never," he had retorted, affection shining in his eyes. "Just get well and get yourself back here before the whole place falls down around me."

Everything had been going according to plan, until she'd made a weekend trip to Boston. Contrary to her hope that her father would react calmly, he had seethed at the news that any man would defile his beautiful young daughter.

"I'll kill the bastard with my bare hands," he roared, his normally pale skin ruddy with anger.

Meghan sighed wearily. She almost wished she hadn't started any of this in the first place, until her hand fell to the small mound of her abdomen.

"Look, Pop. None of this is his fault. I'm a grown woman. I knew the risks, and I'm responsible for my own actions." Seeing the disappointment and disapproval in her father's eyes, she added more gently, "No one is pure and innocent forever, Pop. I'm sorry if I've hurt you."

"Sounds to me like she's taken on the morals of an

alley cat now that she's living in the big city," her brother Donald had commented.

"Shut your mouth," Sean Shay had ordered his son, his attention still on Meghan. "Will the father do the right thing?" he questioned.

The fact that the father didn't know and that she had no intentions of telling him went over like a lead balloon as well.

Her best-loved brother, Connie, was the only one she told the whole truth to. She told him about that night and watched him turn pale with anger and fear.

"Good Lord, Meghan. Where were your brains?" he exploded angrily when she'd finished. "Not only is that the stupidest, most immature thing to do, but it's also a hell of a way to get yourself killed. What an idiot!"

He had reluctantly admitted to understanding her need, but refused to condone her selfish attitude and what she had done. Meghan had left her childhood home in turmoil. She hadn't deluded herself into thinking they'd be overjoyed, but she hadn't been prepared for their condemnation.

Oh, she knew they'd come around and love the baby once it was born; after all, a Shay was a Shay, even under the worst circumstances. But knowing she had hurt and disappointed those she loved most only brought forth another tidal wave of culpability and disgrace.

Pulling her thoughts to earth, she left Central Park and made her way back to the office.

"Any messages, Greta?" she asked.

Greta, a gray-haired woman in her late forties, who was the motherly-type herself, and the most efficient secretary Meghan had worked with, smiled her greeting.

"Henry wants to see you before you leave for the day. Lucy called, but you don't need to call her back. She'll be over tonight," Greta informed her, and then added, "and that woman called."

"What woman?" Meghan asked, smiling at the way Greta had called her "that woman."

"The foreign-speaking female you have in your home now," she clarified indignantly. "I simply dread her calls. It takes forty-five minutes just to find out who she's asking for."

"Oh, it does not," Meghan teased good-naturedly. "Her accent is thick, I'll grant you that, but you should be able to tell by now that when a woman with a thick Polish accent calls this office—on my private line, no less—it's more than likely Mrs. Belinski. What did she need, did she say?"

Greta gave her an obtuse look, and Meghan laughed and asked, "Anything else?"

With a negative shake of her head, Greta prepared to return to her work. Meghan let herself into her office and immediately picked up the receiver and punched out her home phone number.

Mrs. Belinski was the wonderful woman Meghan had hired to be her housekeeper. She was kind, friendly, and cheerful—not to mention the fact that she was a terrific cook. As an added bonus, Mrs. Belinski loved babies and had three grandchildren of her own. A widow, she had agreed to a flexibility that the other applicants couldn't guarantee.

"Yah? Home for Ms. Shay," came across the line.

"Mrs. Belinski? Meghan here. I understand you called the office. Is anything wrong?" Meghan asked.

"Ms. Shay." The voice was suddenly frantic. "They bring di bed of di baby and go. They not take di bed away ven I say."

"That's okay, Mrs. Belinski," she said in a soothing voice. "I ordered a crib earlier this morning. I'm sorry I didn't let you know it was coming."

"Goot. Goot," the older woman said, her tone back to normal. "You want I put away?"

"No. I'll put it away when I get home. Thank you."

Meghan got involved with working on several contracts, and the afternoon slipped by. It was nearly four-thirty before she recalled the message from Henry Alderman.

"Meghan," Henry said in greeting as she entered his office. "I was just getting ready to call and see if you had forgotten me."

"Never, Henry," she replied calmly, although she had.

Henry Alderman was a tall, thin man. He was bald except for a thin fringe of gray hair around the base of his skull, which he kept neatly trimmed. He wore thick, horn-rimmed glasses and spoke in a deep raspy voice. Of all the senior partners in the firm, Meghan liked and respected Henry most. As a junior partner, it was almost a relief to have Henry as her immediate superior. He was a kind, sensitive, honest man, who encouraged those around him to be the same.

"I know you've got a load of work to do right now, but I have another case I'd like you to take on. Actually, it shouldn't be too difficult. It's a fairly cut-and-dried matter, but it's up your alley and could prove to be a good source of future revenue," Henry explained. "If you're not up to it, Gibbs can take it, but I'd rather it got your special attention."

"Why? Who is it? For that matter, what is it?" she asked, showing her interest. Henry had always known just how to work Meghan his way. Or so he thought. In truth, there wasn't anything she wouldn't do for him. She respected him totally and was very fond of him personally.

"Michael Ramsey is his name. He's the eldest son of a Texas oil rancher, and he apparently has set out to make his own fortune. He wants to buy property here and contacted me several weeks ago. The Corbetts recommended us," he said as his phone rang. "So if you could take it on, we'll keep them happy and wind up with a new client," he finished, picking up his phone.

"Yes, Evelyn," he said, then paused. "Fine, put him on." With his eye movements and facial expressions, Henry indicated to Meghan that it was Ramsey on the phone.

"Hello, Mr. Ramsey. I've been expecting your call. . . .

Yes, certainly. That'll be fine. . . . November the twelfth?"
He gave Meghan a questioning look, and she nodded in
answer. "Yes, that will be fine too. . . . No, actually I
won't be. My colleague Ms. Shay will. . . . Oh, the
Corbetts did mention her then. . . . Yes, she is. She's
excellent. . . . Fine, we'll see you then," Henry concluded.

Then as an afterthought he asked, "Mr. Ramsey,
about that other problem you had? Were the investigators able to help you out at all?"

Henry listened intently for several seconds, his expression sympathetic. "No trace of her? I am sorry, Mr.
Ramsey. New York is a big city. . . . Well, if she's still in
New York, Macklin will find her. . . . Well, good luck to
you, and we'll look forward to seeing you on the
twelfth. . . . Good-bye."

Henry shook his head sadly as he replaced the phone
in its cradle.

"What was that last part about?" Meghan inquired,
curious.

Henry eyed her for several seconds distractedly, then
confided, "This poor Ramsey fellow is off his rocker.
When he first contacted me, he also asked for the name
of a reliable investigator for a personal problem he was
having. I gave him Macklin's name and number and
told him Macklin was the best.

"About a month after that, Macklin called me and
wanted to know what I knew about Ramsey. Apparently Ramsey met a woman the last time he was here,
and somehow lost contact with her. Macklin didn't tell
me all the details, but he did say that all Ramsey gave
him to go on was a composite sketch of the woman,
her first name, and a few vague leads.

"When Macklin reported to him that he wasn't able
to find her, Ramsey told him to check everywhere,
including the underworld, because there could be a
chance the woman was in some sort of danger. It seems
he met her under a strange set of circumstances, and
poor Ramsey was worried sick about her. Macklin didn't

want to take unnecessary chances in the dirty money circles if Ramsey were some sort of nut who went around finding homes for lost women or something, so he called me for a reference."

Henry sat quietly, obviously thinking about the hopelessness of Ramsey's quest.

"Well? Is he?" Meghan asked, burning with curiosity about her newest client.

"Is he what?" asked Henry, returning his attention to the conversation.

"Is he a nut?" she specified.

"No. I don't think so," he said reflectively. "I think he just wants to find this woman." Henry laughed suddenly, and in answer to Meghan's expectant expression explained, "He said that when he did find her, he was going to wring her neck for disappearing and putting him through all this. Now, does that sound like a nut to you?"

That evening when Meghan got home, Mrs. Belinski was still there waiting for her.

"I leave your supper in di oven. You eat now. Will not be too done," she said after Meghan had hung up her coat and turned to the woman, puzzled.

Mrs. Belinski wiped her clean, dry hands nervously on her apron, then went into the kitchen to retrieve Meghan's dinner. After Meghan was seated at the breakfast bar, her meal before her, the older woman cleared her throat several times before she spoke.

"I don't ask anything when di paper with di fuzzy ducks come. I don't ask anything when di lovely rocking chair come. But I think I should now." She hesitated briefly, then got to the point. "You be with di baby, yah?"

"Yes, Mrs. Belinski," Meghan stated calmly.

The silence was deafening. Mrs. Belinski obviously had a million questions she didn't know how to ask, and Meghan was dreading them. "Now that you know, Mrs. Belinski, will you be staying on or would you rather not," Meghan asked, her pride shielding her from the woman's reaction.

"Yah. Yah. I stay. I tell you always I love di little ones," she said cheerfully. "I ask something?" With Meghan's silent consent she asked, "When does di baby come?"

"The first of April," the mother-to-be supplied, waiting for the next question.

Her eyes twinkling, the older woman asked, "You wish for di little boy or di little girl?"

Hiring the housekeeper for the baby, arranging the leave of absence, preparing the spare bedroom for the baby, and keeping her pregnancy under wraps were all part of phase two of Meghan's grand plan.

With Mrs. Belinski's acceptance, Meghan felt relatively content and happy that all was going well.

Four

Mid-November found New York colder and more windy.
It had snowed the night before, but by the morning,
the soft, fluffy whiteness had turned to gray-black slush
in the streets and on the sidewalks. Michael surveyed
the mess from the window of Henry Alderman's office.

"Macklin hasn't turned up anything then?" Henry
asked.

"Nothing. It's been four months, and I even had him
hire extra men in Boston. I just don't think she's in
New York anymore," Michael said dejectedly. "And I
wouldn't know where to start looking outside the two
cities."

"I suppose Macklin looked into the possibility that
she was just another guest in the hotel," Henry stated,
knowing that he probably had.

"Oh, yes. He tried everything," Michael said, turning
from the window. "I just think it's time to hang this
one up and go on. She obviously didn't want me to
know who she was, or she'd have told me."

"I'm sorry. But you're probably right. She could be
anywhere."

That same phrase had echoed through Michael's head
for months. A dozen times he was tempted to call off

46

the search, when out of despair a new possibility would arise. But enough was enough. This afternoon he'd pay off Macklin, and even if she continued to plague his thoughts, he was determined to get on with his life. After all, it's not as if she were his missing mother or wife—or even anybody he knew. She was just . . . that woman. That woman who had come to him out of nowhere. That intriguing woman who was so beautiful, so passionate . . . and in the end so strangely sad. Lately, he had even been considering the fact that she might not have been real after all. That maybe she was only a fatigue-induced fantasy.

Michael sighed loudly and ran his hand through his dark hair in frustration. With great effort, he attempted to lighten his mood.

"Speaking of lost women, do you suppose your associate will be much longer?" he asked, grinning. "My luck with women lately has led me to become very nervous when they don't show up when I expect them to."

Henry chuckled appreciatively. "You can relax on that score with Meghan. She's as reliable as they come. She's been in court all week with a tricky suit we filed for a client. She was supposed to finish it up this morning."

"I understood yesterday when I called to confirm our appointment that she could be a little late. And I came early hoping for the chance to meet you and thank you for the help and concern you've given me with the problem of my missing lady. You're very kind."

"Not at all," Henry said self-consciously. "I wish I could have done more. Now, let me check on Meghan for you, and we'll get started on something that should be a lot easier and more pleasant to take care of."

When Alderman opened his office door, a flash of red caught the attention of both men. Michael went rigid with shock as he watched a shapely red-headed woman take several steps and enter another office across the reception area. As Macklin had pointed out to him time after time, there were thousands of red-haired women in New York, but Michael would bet his life that only one could walk like that.

He had found her. After four months of worrying himself sick about her. After thousands of dollars of investigators' fees. After . . . after everything else she'd put him through, there she was. Pretty as you please. Safe and sound. Every emotion Michael had felt over the last few months came to a head inside him, completely bypassing relief and turning to boiling anger.

"Ah, speaking of the devil, there she goes. Come along and I'll introduce the two of you," Henry said cheerfully, oblivious to the fact that Michael was working on a catalog of the various means by which he planned to take his revenge.

The unsuspecting Meghan was just settling behind her desk when there was a brief knock on the door. Henry let himself in, saying, "Meghan. You're back. How did it go this morning?"

"Fine. I—" Meghan's whole world stopped short when she spied the man who had followed Henry into her office. The room went suddenly dark. Her heart stood still. The color the wind had blown into her cheeks drained away. Her eyes grew large, then snapped shut in an unconscious attempt at self-preservation, as if closing out the sight of him would allow her lungs to take in the air she needed to breathe.

Michael enjoyed her reaction tremendously, but it only whetted his appetite.

"Meghan," broke in Henry's startled voice. "Are you all right? Have you seen Lucy lately? Can I get you anything?"

Meghan was nodding and shaking her head furiously in response to his rapid-fire questions, but she couldn't speak. She had to concentrate on staying alive.

"Ms. Shay," came a deep baritone. "You look as if you're had a terrible shock. Is something wrong?"

The added impact of his voice jolted the air from her lungs, and her emergency life-support system kicked in. She opened her eyes slowly. Immediately, she could see the man was having a very good time at her expense.

He was casually leaning against the doorjamb of her office. With supreme control, he held the laughter in his throat at bay, but his eyes were another story. They were sparkling wildly, laughing exultantly.

For generations, the Shays had had nothing to claim but pride. And Meghan Shay had inherited her share. Determinedly, she straightened her spine and puffed out her chest. Her chin came up defiantly, but she couldn't quite look him in the eye.

"I'm fine, Henry," she said, and cleared her throat. Then, since no Shay ever died sitting down, she rose to a standing position and added, "Lucy said I need to get more rest. You must be Mr. Ramsey."

"Oh, sorry," Henry apologized. "Meghan Shay. Michael Ramsey."

"How do you do, Mr. Ramsey. Would you like to sit down?" she asked, sending up yet another silent prayer of thanks for all those poker lessons.

"What does the M stand for?" Michael asked with pleasant enough curiosity. He indicated the name printed on her office door, which still stood ajar.

As Michael made his way across the office and took a chair directly in front of Meghan's desk, Henry answered him. "Mary. The M stands for Mary. Mary Meghan Shay just drips of saints and virgins, doesn't it?" Henry teased her, as he had a thousand times before.

"Certainly does," Michael agreed, his voice cracking with laughter. Giving Meghan a meaningful look, he repeated slowly, "Saints and virgins."

Blissfully, Henry continued to dig Meghan's hole as he retold the old office joke about her name. "We were a little surprised when she used an initial for Mary. We always thought it made her sound so incorruptible that it would have made great public relations for the firm."

Michael laughed appropriately for Henry, but his rebuttal was for Meghan. "It would indeed. But we all know actions speak louder than words. I'm sure Ms. Shay's reputation says more about her skills than her name does."

When Meghan gasped, Michael was delighted with his direct hit.

She shuffled papers around on her desk in embarrassment, trying to settle herself.

Meghan was panic-stricken, but the emotion she felt most intensely was pain. She deserved his anger and ridicule, and she knew it, but it hurt nonetheless. She blinked back the tears that welled in her eyes as she pushed papers back and forth on her desk. All she could do was handle the situation with as much dignity as she had left.

With a strange glint in her eyes that Michael couldn't decipher, she looked straight at him and said, "Mr. Ramsey's right, Henry," then she changed the subject. "I understand you're buying a piece of the Apple, Mr. Ramsey."

"Yes, I am," he stated. "Since it's so close to noon, perhaps we could discuss it over lunch, say . . . at the Essex," he zinged her again, then for Henry's benefit he added, "I'm staying there and have an appointment there later, so it would be convenient, and the food is excellent."

"Thank you," she said softly. "But I have an appointment with my doctor at one-thirty. So, if you wouldn't mind, we can discuss it now."

At this point, Henry the Helpful decided to go.

"Mr. Ramsey, I'll leave you now in Meghan's expert hands. I'm glad we got the chance to meet."

"The pleasure was mine, Mr. Alderman, and please

call me Michael. I have a feeling my attorney and I will be in conference often, and I'm hoping we can run into each other again sometime," he said, as he rose to shake Henry's hand.

"I'll look forward to it, Michael, and you can call me Henry. I'm sure you will find Meghan is the best there is for this sort of affair," he said, before letting himself out of the room.

Michael stared after him in amused wonder. Then, calling his own temporary truce with Meghan, he turned and gave her a wry grin. "He wasn't much help to you, was he?"

"He meant well," she retorted with a shrug.

"That's true," he conceded, the truce over. "Now, can we say the same for you?"

Meghan decided there were too many potholes in the road ahead and tried to steer clear of them.

"Shall we discuss your acquisition, Mr. Ramsey?" she asked formally.

"Ah," he said, as if suddenly enlightened. "We're all business in the daylight hours too."

"That's up to you, Mr. Ramsey. I'm leaving at one o'clock. You can sit there and torture me until then if you want to. However, you will be charged for my time, and we won't be any closer to reaching a settlement on your property. The choice is yours," she pointed out tersely, sitting down in her chair and crossing her legs comfortably.

"Oh, good. Then my choice *does* occasionally matter," he said sarcastically. He opened his briefcase and brought out a file folder. He flipped it carelessly onto the top of her desk.

"I have a verbal agreement to buy out Dobson Publishing Company," he began in a professional tone as cold as her own. "I want total ownership, complete rights, and the use of their good name for as long as I own the company. In return for which I will give them their total asking price. I then wish to have the necessary papers drawn up to incorporate it into Texacal. Their attorneys' names and addresses as well as those of my attorneys in Texas, and several other minor stipulations, are listed in there also."

His instructions were clear to Meghan and left her with nothing to say. He closed his briefcase, latched it, and stood to leave, saying, "If you have any questions, you know where to reach me."

At the door he turned to study her intently, then cautioned her, "I'm not through with you, Meghan Shay."

She returned his steady look and uttered, "I didn't think you were, Mr. Ramsey."

Meghan's appointment with her doctor took place over lunch in an Italian restaurant that Meghan and Lucy often frequented.

"Oh Lord, Meghan, what are you going to do?" asked a terrified Lucy after listening to the horrifying story.

Morose, Meghan shrugged and glanced across the table at her friend. "I don't know," she stated dully, then as an afterthought added, "You don't happen to have a bottle of pills I could take?"

"Meghan," Lucy gasped.

The red-haired mother-to-be propped her elbow on the table and laid her forehead in her hand. "Relax," she mumbled. "It was just the first thing that came to mind. You know I'd never do anything to harm the baby."

"Oh Lord, Meghan," Lucy repeated, for at least the tenth time since their meal was served.

Peeking through her fingers at Lucy, Meghan released a derisive half laugh and offered, "Just imagine what he'd say if he found out I'm pregnant."

"Oh Lord, Meghan!"

Lucy's remark drew the attention of some of the other diners. Glancing around at the onlookers and then back to one another, the women broke into giggles. The tension effectively drained from the conversation, Lucy encouraged Meghan to eat some of her untouched meal.

After two or three small, tasteless bites of superb manicotti, Meghan began to play with the cherry tomato in her salad. Thoughtfully turning it over and over with her fork, she finally muttered, "There isn't anything I can do."

Lucy watched her, but didn't speak.

"I'll just avoid him when I can and endure him when I can't," she concluded. "Let's face it, Luce, I deserve it. Somewhere in that panic this morning, I actually felt relief. I remember thinking, 'Oh, good. He's come to kill me and I won't feel guilty anymore!' What I did to him is appalling. What I should do," she stated vehemently, "is confess the whole thing and let him horsewhip me until we both feel better."

"Meghan," Lucy said sympathetically.

Meghan heaved a heavy sigh.

"Look, Meg, avoid him like you said before. Eventually he'll either run out of nasty things to say or he'll go back to Texas. It can't go on forever," consoled the eternal optimist.

Meghan looked at Lucy as if she were suddenly inspired with a superior idea.

"That's it, Lucy." Meghan grinned exultantly. "He'll leave soon. And if he doesn't, I'll be leaving in a month or so anyway. If I can be pregnant for nine months, I can surely put up with him for one. At least he doesn't make me nauseous," she said, giggling. "Speaking of nausea, when will that go away? Greta's not stupid, you know. If she catches me as pale as a ghost with a mouth full of crackers again, she's going to start getting a little suspicious."

Greta was suspicious, but not of Meghan's physical condition.

"That big hunk of Texas called while you were out," she reported, when the young attorney returned to her office.

"What big hunk of Texas?" Meghan inquired too casually.

"Well, how many big hunks of Texas have you met lately?" the older woman wanted to know.

Meghan's gaze wandered around the room as she tried to recall the exact number.

After several seconds, Greta supplied the answer for herself.

"Michael Ramsey."

"Oh. What did he want?"

"He wanted you to call him when you got back from your doctor's appointment," Greta relayed.

"Oh," was Meghan's response.

"I didn't realize you had another appointment to see Lucy this afternoon," a concerned Greta said, hoping for more information on Meghan's health.

"We . . . we had lunch at Tonio's," she mumbled guiltily. She left instructions to tell all callers she'd left for the day to work on a pile of paperwork that had to be cleared up by Monday. Then she walked as nonchalantly as possible into her office and closed the door.

She didn't hear Greta murmur a knowing, "I see."

Five

That weekend wouldn't go down as one of Meghan's favorites.

She stayed in the entire time, sure that now that lightning had already struck once, a second time was entirely possible.

She worked on a couple of cases she'd brought home from the office. She watched television absently. She read the first page of the same book twice and finally tossed it onto the coffee table beside one of her cooked and recooked TV dinners—not her favorite fare.

Her answering machine had been on all weekend, but on Sunday morning she took Lucy's call and one from Connie, who inquired about her health and offered his help if she needed it. Put out with her, it was his way of letting her know he still loved her.

She didn't, however, return any of the calls Michael Ramsey ordered her to. Not the Friday night call when he said, "I'll pretend that I think you didn't go back to the office this afternoon. Please call me when you get home."

The Saturday morning call was a little nasty. Why should she answer, "Unless you were out working on another thesis last night, I'm sure you eventually got

my message. I'm still waiting for your call." In the
afternoon his call was slightly threatening, "Meghan. I
have the patience of Job, but don't push me." Meghan
was too nervous to call after that. Later that night she
realized the afternoon call was nothing compared to
the one he made at ten-thirty. "Dammit, Meghan! Call
me!"

Michael's last call came on Sunday afternoon, and
Meghan's heart fluttered with anxiety when he informed
her calmly, "I'll be calling you at the office in the morning, Meghan. If you don't take my call, I'll be over in
person. If you call in sick tomorrow, I may have to have
a talk with my friend Henry and tell him you're avoiding my calls. . . . Talk to you *soon*, darlin'."

Monday morning she was in the office for Michael's
call.

"Yes, Mr. Ramsey," she greeted him cheerfully.

Before she could say anything else, he broke in angrily, "Why the hell didn't you answer my messages?"

"I am sorry, Mr. Ramsey. I did get all of your . . . kind
messages, but the last one led me to believe that rather
than return your call last night, you preferred to call
me here this morning." Hesitant, she then added coyly,
"Isn't that right, Mr. Ramsey?"

Silence.

"Mr. Ramsey?"

"Meghan," he said semisweetly. "I've kissed the little
freckle you carry low on your left hip . . . and then
some. So don't you think you ought to call me Michael?
Henry does, and I haven't been nearly as familiar with
him."

"Very well, Michael, if that's what you want. Was
there anything else you wanted to discuss?" she asked
innocently.

She could hear him breathing heavily on the other
end of the line, but he didn't speak.

"Michael? Was that all you wanted?" she repeated.

"No! That's not all I wanted. I want you to go out to
dinner with me," he said testily.

"What a kind invitation, Michael," she cooed. "Is this business or pleasure?"

"Would 'pleasure' get you there?" he asked cautiously.

"I don't go out with clients, Michael," she said purposefully.

"Then it's business," he said through gritted teeth.

"Oh. Well in that case, I do have a couple of free hours this afternoon if you would like to come in—"

"Meghan," he interrupted. "I do not want to come into your office. And I think I ought to let you know I'm near the end of my rope."

She laughed softly and confided, "You know, Michael, I never would have dreamed that someone from Texas could ever run out of rope. However, if tomorrow would be more convenient for—"

"Dammit, Meghan!" he bellowed, and then there was silence on both ends. Finally, as if speaking to the village idiot, he said, "Meghan, darlin', I'd rather not have to threaten you to get you to have dinner with me, but I promise you, if you don't come out with me, I'm going to spend the entire night thinking up something really terrible to do to you."

Meghan sighed loudly, fatigued from the battle of wills. Seeing herself as the loser in this skirmish, she gave one more valiant try.

"Michael," she said, her voice pleading for mercy. "We'll be working together fairly often over the next month or so. I promise you'll have plenty of time to browbeat me. Couldn't we just leave it at that?"

There was silence for what seemed like an eternity before Michael said slowly, "What if I don't? What if we call a truce?"

"A truce?" she asked, stunned by his sudden turn-around.

"Yes, counselor. It's like a contract . . . a pact. A deal not to fight anymore."

"A truce," she clarified.

"Yeah. How about it?"

"I'd like that," she said, truly grateful.

"Then can we have dinner together tonight?" he asked with assurance.

"Well, I . . . well . . . could . . . could we make it Thursday instead?" she asked, playing for time. The longer she could avoid him, the better. If they could make it Thursday, she'd have only three weeks to go before she left town.

"Thursday?" he exclaimed, his voice rising again.

"I'm sorry, Michael. I . . . I . . ."

"Thursday," he broke in. "Eight o'clock. I'll pick you up."

"Oh. I could just meet you. You don't—"

"I'll pick you up," he reiterated.

"Fine."

The week whizzed by. At seven fifty-five on Thursday night Meghan was totally dressed, totally petrified, and totally nauseous.

Her forehead and the back of her neck were moist with perspiration. She was sure her face looked as pale as chalk. But she was as ready as she'd ever be. She had cleverly chosen a moss green evening dress that was lined in taffeta. In two pieces, the flowing blouson top had a drop waist and side hip band trimmed in pearls. The skirt was comfortable and extremely becoming with its elasticized waistband to conceal her pregnancy and the pleats to flatter her figure.

An unsavory saltiness seeped into Meghan's mouth as she waited anxiously for Michael to arrive. At this point in her pregnancy she knew all the signs of an imminent eruption and made a mad dash for her crackers. Not in their usual place, Meghan cursed the lovable Mrs. Belinski and started flinging open cupboards and drawers as the doorbell chimed.

"Oh Lord," she moaned dejectedly, swallowing a mouthful of saliva, hoping it would stay down—hoping everything would stay down—as she went to greet Michael.

Throwing open the door, she instantly and swiftly retraced her steps back to the kitchen, blurting out, "Come in and sit down," as the contents of her stomach bounced erratically between her abdomen and the back of her throat.

A bewildered Michael stepped cautiously into Meghan's cheerful apartment and quietly closed the door. Entering the living room, he guessed she had disappeared into the kitchen, because from around the corner came a conspicuous barrage of crashes and clangs and resounding clatter. Through the din he thought he heard a string of low-spoken expletives, but when the clamor finally ceased, Meghan walked calmly and slowly into the room and leaned serenely, and to Michael's eye very seductively, against the wall.

Aside from the fact that she was a little pale, more than likely from nerves, she looked ravishing, and Michael's heart began to beat at a rapid-fire pace.

"Hi," she croaked softly, giving him a nervous smile. "Are you ready to go?"

"Sure . . . unless you'd rather have a drink here and relax a little bit first. We have lots of time," he offered obligingly.

"A drink?" she asked blankly, her mind-over-matter delusion needing her full concentration.

"Yes, a drink. Usually it's some sort of fluid . . . in a glass or a cup. I'm not picky," he said graciously. "Water is fine. Or tea or coffee. Even vegetable juice." He paused, watching her curiously. "Anything but oyster juice," he said. "I'm not overly fond of oyster juice."

"Oyster juice?" she pronounced, her beautifully green and expressive eyes staring at him woefully.

"Yeah," he said, baffled by her strange reactions. "In fact," he went on, "about the only things I absolutely refuse to put in my mouth are oyster juice, cow tongue, and sushi."

"Oh Lord, Michael!" she spat out in disgust as she raced into the bedroom.

After several minutes of kicking his heels around in the living room, completely disoriented by the situation, Michael wondered if he ought to check on her—maybe apologize for something.

Hanging over the toilet, a disgruntled Meghan tossed what she hoped was her last cracker and sighed deeply.

"Meghan? Are you all right," came Michael's deep baritone voice through the door.

"I'll be fine," she called, jumping up dizzily to turn on the shower, which would muffle any noises she made. "Just go, Michael. Go into the kitchen and drink anything you like," she said, and then as an afterthought added, "If you see anything you're not . . . overly fond of, just . . . put it in the garbage," she managed to say before she belched reminiscently.

She assumed Michael had gone in search of a drink, because he didn't say anything else. She stretched out on the cool tiles of the bathroom floor until the nausea and light-headedness subsided. Slowly, she brought herself back to a standing position. Not one to be overly concerned with her looks when death was threatening, she splashed cold water on her face and patted it dry. Taking deep, calming breaths, she turned off the shower and moved to the door, wondering how on earth she'd ever explain this to Michael.

Michael had drawn his own conclusions. Meghan found him sitting on her bed waiting for her.

"A little under the weather, huh?" he said sympathetically, kindness and concern etched on his face. His gray eyes examined her astutely as she held onto the doorjamb for support. "Must be the flu. It's that season," he deduced.

"Lucy says there's a lot of it going around," she muttered, nodding in agreement. It was better than anything her foggy brain had come up with.

"Poor thing. Come here, and I'll help you get into bed," he commiserated. As he stood, she saw he was holding an old flannel nightgown that had been buried so far down in her dresser, she'd forgotten she had it. As she looked from the gown to her dresser, he explained unselfconsciously, "It'll keep you warmer than the others. Come here."

Reluctantly, she went to him. If he brought out his horsewhip now, she'd be too weak to stop him, she thought.

He turned her away from him and began to draw down the zipper at the back of her neck. She spun around, clutching her dress to her, panic rising to temporarily replace her nausea.

"Don't be silly, Meghan," he said wryly. "I've already seen all there is to see."

That's what you think, she said to herself.

"And I've never before attacked a woman on her deathbed," he finished, turning her again. As he unzipped her dress, he murmured, "Of course, there's a first time for everything."

When she jerked around to face him once again, fear and outrage in her green eyes, he laughed deep and low in his throat and grinned at her charmingly.

"I'm teasing, Meghan," he said in a soothing voice as he began to peel her clothes away. He held her flannel gown while she wiggled into it, and when she had finished, he turned her around and buttoned up the opening in back.

"I'll do that," he informed her, as she started to hang up her dress. Ordinarily she wouldn't have bothered, but she'd paid a small fortune for this bit of designer camouflage and thought it might be worth taking care of.

With Meghan in bed, Michael placed a cool, damp cloth over her forehead and tucked the blanket up around her neck. He regarded her with concern for several minutes, then started to leave the room. "Be right back," he said over his shoulder.

In the kitchen he pondered the tricks one's mind could play. He had thought he'd remembered her body as well as he knew his own, but his memory hadn't recalled her being quite so full breasted, and her formerly flat abdomen was in actuality just slightly rounded. Neither error made much difference. She was still as incredibly lovely as she had been in all his dreams.

Meghan was feeling perfectly well by now, but her heart and mind were racing a mile a minute. She marveled at the way his most casual touch affected her. Her whole body was tingling with excitement. Aside from the fact that she hadn't gone out with anyone since the night she'd met Michael, no one before that had ever made her feel this way. Actually, it was a little frightening.

Michael entered the room again. "Would you like me to stay on the couch tonight? In case you need anything?" he offered, placing a glass of water on her bedside table.

"Oh, no," she said, alarmed. "I . . . I just like being left alone when I'm ill. Thank you, anyway. And I'm . . . sorry about our date."

"I'm just sorry I didn't notice how sick and pale you were," he confessed.

"Don't feel bad, please. It's my hair."

"Your hair?" he repeated stupidly.

"Uh-huh. Redheads are notoriously pale. And when pale gets paler, it's still just pale," she explained, as if it made perfect sense.

"I see. Well, that makes me feel a little better, anyway," he said, his lips twitching into an amused grin. "If you don't want me to stay, will you at least make me a promise?"

"Sure," she said amiably.

"Call me if there's anything you need, or anything I can do to help," he said, indicating that the paper he laid beside her phone had his number on it.

"I promise," she vowed.

He leaned over and dropped a warm, sweet kiss on her forehead, replaced the cloth, and stood grinning down on her.

"I'm taking a rain check on our dinner, Meghan. You get well quickly," he ordered.

She returned his grin brilliantly and promised, "I will and . . . thank you, Michael."

"Good night, Meghan."

"Good night."

Michael left the light in the hall burning because it shed enough of a glow to illuminate most of her apartment.

He scanned her living room trying to glean more information about her. It was a neat, tidy, and impeccably clean room. He added domestic to his list of details about her.

On a table near one of the chairs he spied three photographs. One of an older couple and a young woman, which didn't offer much information other than that all three were blond. The second picture was of Meghan and three red-headed men. One man was older, and his hair, like the others, was the identical shade of Meghan's, but was showing signs of gray. Her family.

The last picture was older than the others. It depicted a blond woman, who looked remarkably like Meghan, and the red-headed man, looking years younger, from the previous picture. Her parents, he realized.

What a treasure chest he'd found. She was sentimental, devoted to family, and came from a line of red-haired, green-eyed kinsmen.

Well, that was enough to go on for now. It was more than he'd known a week ago.

"Michael? Are you still here?" came Meghan's tired voice.

"Yes," he whispered guiltily, as he went down the

hall again and stuck his head into the room. "It occurred to me you might want an aspirin or something to settle your stomach." He'd always been quick on his feet, he thought gratefully.

"No. Thank you," she whispered back. "I don't take any kind of medication, except some vitamins that Lucy gives me. I usually just ride these illnesses out."

"Well, okay then, good night," he said, as he added "health conscious" to his list of Meghan's traits and left the apartment.

Meghan breathed a sigh of relief when she finally heard the door close softly and latch itself. She'd listened to him prowling around out there and had held her breath. From his tone, he had obviously found nothing questionable and Meghan thanked the heavens for her continued good fortune.

Ambiguity reigned again as she was torn between the joy of her good luck and the disgrace of continuing to deceive Michael. He had been so kind and gentle. It amazed her that such a Goliath of a man could be so tender and comforting. He was a charming man, and Meghan felt really sad about having to get rid of him somehow.

She snuggled under the covers and put her mind to other, more immediate problems—such as how could she drag her nonexistent flu out for the next three weeks without Michael getting suspicious?

Six

Meghan called in sick on Friday as part of her ploy. She did, however, finish some work she'd brought home with her. One of those cases was Michael's. She made several calls regarding the matter, and phoned Greta to request that some additional information be gathered for her by Monday. Shortly after noon when Michael called to check on her, she told him she was better but still a little woozy when she got out of bed.

Not quite an hour later, there was a soft knock at her door seconds before her doorbell chimed. Frowning, Meghan went to the door and called, "Who is it, please?"

"Michael."

"One minute, Michael," she stalled. And that was all it took to scoop up her files, run down the hall, and throw them in the spare room. She shucked her sweatpants and T-shirt and climbed into her robe, messing her hair and adopting a haggard look as she headed back to the door.

She shook her arms to loosen her muscles, slouched her shoulders, and tried to look pathetic as she peered around the door at Michael.

"Oh. Hi, Michael," she greeted him weakly.

"Hi. You look as awful as you sounded on the phone,

poor darlin'," he graciously commented with concern. "May I come in? I've brought you something."

"I don't know, Michael." She hesitated. "I wouldn't want you to catch my bug." She pulled her head back to cough disgustingly into the sleeve of her terry robe.

"Impossible," Michael said confidently. "I never catch stuff like that. I'm as healthy as an ox," he assured her.

"Well, maybe in Texas. But this is New York. We have very potent germs here," she warned him.

"Maybe, but ours are probably bigger and stronger, so it all evens out in the end, I imagine," he said, grinning. "Are you going to let me in, or am I going to have to force the door open?"

Meghan had to admit that in all likelihood, his chances of catching her particular condition *were* impossible, and her chances of getting him to go away were just about as good. So with a weary sigh, she widened the gap in the door, allowing him to enter.

"If you brought me chocolates, I think I should warn you that my throat is all raw, and I probably won't be able to eat them," she whined peevishly as she thought a sick person might.

"Much better than chocolate when you're sick is my mother's beef broth," he informed her cheerfully, ignoring her distemper. "I think you call it bouillon up here, at least that's what the chef at the Essex called it when I gave him the recipe," he said, heading for her kitchen.

"You called your mother for her recipe for beef broth?" she asked, so amazed she forgot to sound sick, as she followed him into the kitchen.

"Sure did," he said over his shoulder, looking for a pot. "And you'll thank me someday, because it'll get you back on your feet and feeling as healthy as a horse."

Meghan thought it appropriate that a Texan would think it took beef broth to make you feel like a horse, but she kept it to herself. Her thoughts and emotions in turmoil, she felt like a piece of gum stuck to the sole of somebody's shoe. This huge man was so innately good and kind, he could kill her with guilt and shame. Her eyes began to fill with tears, and her heart was heavy with remorse. Why couldn't things be different?

"This'll fix up those watery eyes too," he said sympathetically. "You go sit down and I'll bring this in to you."

"You really don't need to wait on me," she protested. "You've gone to too much trouble as it is."

"Liberated women," he said irreverently with a shake of his big, dark head. "You'll do yourselves in if you don't let people help you once in a while."

Too weary to argue the point, Meghan shuffled off to the couch. Plopping down onto the cushions, she drew her feet up and tucked her robe around them. *How was she going to get out of this one?* she asked herself with a heavy sigh. "Tell him," her conscience told her emphatically. "Tell him and get it over with." Meghan knew it was good advice and she wanted to use it, but she knew she wouldn't, couldn't today. Why did he have to be so nice? It was very hard being cruel to a nice person, she concluded miserably. And she knew that whichever road she eventually took, Michael was bound to be hurt.

"Here ya go," he said, carefully carrying the bowl of thin soup and placing it in her lap. "Now eat up while it's hot."

Spoonful after tasteless spoonful, Meghan ate, aware only of the man sitting beside her watching her solicitously, and the jangling of her nerves that grew stronger with each mouthful. She slid him a quick glance and saw he was smiling in a very self-satisfied way.

"Feeling better, aren't you?" he asked, confident of her answer. "I told you that would do the trick. Even the color in your face is better."

It was Meghan's guess that he could make a rutabaga turn pink if he stared at it long enough.

"It was very good. Thank you. And thank you for all

the trouble you went to, but it wasn't really necessary," she said, wishing he'd leave now that his act of charity had been completed. "I'm quite capable of taking care of myself."

He grinned. "I know you are, but don't forget, I have a vested interest in you. I personally want to make sure you get well quickly. I brought enough soup for a couple of days, and I'll come by to . . ."

"Oh, no. Please," she pleaded. "Don't come again." Seeing his sudden frown, she explained, "I . . . I'm not a very nice sick person and having people around only makes me feel uncomfortable and embarrassed. Please, it was very kind of you to bring your mother's beef broth, and I'll certainly eat it, but I'd really rather be alone."

Michael considered her request for several seconds, then bargained, "Can I at least call and check on you?"

"Yes, of course." Meghan sighed with relief. "But you don't need to. I'll be fine in no time."

"I want to," he stated firmly, rising. "Get plenty of rest, you look a little strung out," he added with concern.

Meghan just nodded, hoping he would go away. She'd agree to almost anything to get him to leave. Again, the idea of simply blurting the whole story out to him crossed her mind. Surely his anger would be easier to cope with than his benevolence.

She followed him to the door, anxious to hasten his departure.

Michael turned to face her at the door. His big hands came forward, and he gently took her by the shoulders. He studied her intently before he finally placed a tender, heart-quickening kiss on her forehead.

"I'll call you later," he promised, then opened the door and left.

Meghan fell back heavily against the door. She blew the hair off her face and rolled her eyes heavenward. "I can imagine how unhappy you are with me right about now. But if you could help me out a little here, I'd sure appreciate it," she prayed aloud.

Saturday morning she tempted the fates with a quick trip to her gym. She ran several of what Lucy called gentle jogs around the track, and worked with some passive machines before going home. This time when Michael called she was up and around a little more, but still weak and frayed around the edges. When he mentioned that he knew she must be feeling a little better because her phone was busy earlier, she simply said that Lucy phoned frequently to check on her too.

Sunday she felt much stronger and thought if she rested well, she might make it into work the next day.

"Good," said Michael encouragingly. "I'll call you and see how you feel. Maybe you'll be up to going out for a bowl of gruel or something."

"Michael, let me call you. I've been sort of glancing through some of my papers here, and I need to check on a few more things regarding your purchase. I'll call you, and we can discuss some of them and maybe work out a day for that dinner too," she said.

"All right," he agreed slowly. "But there's no maybe about it. Eventually you and I are going to have a nice long talk, and it won't be about anything vaguely associated with the law."

The next day she waited until mid-afternoon to phone Michael.

"Michael? Meghan Shay," she said in greeting.

"Meghan," he said cheerfully. "I'm glad to hear from you . . . at last," he added pointedly. How many times today had he picked up the phone to call her only to lay it down again, telling himself it was important to trust that she'd call him if she said she would? He'd been obsessed with the woman since he'd met her. She was on his mind constantly, and yet . . . he didn't mind it at all. He enjoyed thinking about her. How had she gotten under his skin so quickly? His tough bachelor's hide had become very thin since she'd come into his life, and it felt terrific and frightening at the same time.

"Sorry, Michael. But you wouldn't want an attorney who didn't know all the facts, would you?" she said, cajoling him.

"I'll let that one pass, Meghan," he said, his tone lightening. "So. Do we discuss business or pleasure first?"

"Let's get business out of the way," she said, opting for firmer ground.

"Okay."

"Actually, Henry was right; this case is fairly cut and dried. All your stipulations have been agreed to, and their attorneys are cooperating wonderfully. It's just . . . well, it's . . . I don't even know how to put this," she faltered, trying not to offend him.

"Pretend the question has something to do with venereal disease or my fertility," he quipped, enjoying himself.

The aftermath of Michael's bomb was deafening silence.

"Meghan?" he called cautiously. "It was supposed to be a joke. I'm sorry."

"Listen, Mr. Ramsey," she said coolly. "I don't know how they do things in Texas, but where I'm from, a truce is a truce. You don't make up your own rules as you go." Hoping he felt like fighting back, Meghan thought this might be a good way of getting out of dinner.

"I said I was sorry, Meghan," he said in repentance.

Rats! she thought. "What I wanted to say," she started, "was that I've been doing some checking. Dobson's is an extremely solvent company and basically a good buy . . ."

"Thank you," he interrupted.

". . . but even taking into consideration the fact that

you're buying the rights to the name," she went on without hesitation, "the asking price you're willing to pay is ridiculously high. Are you sure you wouldn't like to do a little dickering here?" she finished.

"Have you met the Dobson brothers yet?" Michael asked indulgently.

"No."

"Well, when you do, you'll find that what they're asking, in my opinion anyway, isn't nearly what they ought to ask for."

"Why?" she questioned, her curiosity piqued.

"These two old guys started a neighborhood newspaper to sell to their friends when they were ten and six years old. The older one was a good student and a little shy as a boy, so he did all the writing. The younger brother was an extroverted go-getter. He went out and brought back all the news.

"Later they both got jobs on newspapers and after several years set out on their own. They hocked everything, and for years they and their young wives and babies lived on practically nothing in order to get *Citizen's Magazine* off the ground.

"The rest of their story is mostly about a hell of a lot of hard work and the struggles they fought to maintain the integrity of their publications, which, as you know, now number eight separate magazines and periodicals.

"I honestly don't think what they're asking is too much to pay for the fruits of their endeavors, for the use of their good name, or for two old men's lifework. So I'll pay it," he said, finishing his story on a note of admiration.

Meghan was silent for a while, considering the man Michael Ramsey was. Her heart swelled with pride.

"Have you ever been poor and had to struggle, Michael?" she asked, wondering at his empathy.

"No." He chuckled good-naturedly. "My dad had things pretty well set from as far back as I can remember. But he and my mother lived through some tough times.

They don't take anything they have for granted, and they wouldn't let their children either." He laughed in remembrance.

"We can talk more about it over dinner tonight," he said, smoothly leading into a subject closer to his heart.

"Tonight?" she stalled.

"Are you up to it?" he asked, trusting soul that he was.

"I am a little tired, but how about Wednesday or Thursday?" she suggested deceptively.

"How about tomorrow night?" he offered.

"Tomorrow's Tuesday," she pointed out.

"Yes, I know. Don't they serve dinner in New York on Tuesdays?"

She giggled. "I'm not sure. I always go to see Jeff on Tuesday."

"Jeff?" he questioned, sounding calmer than he felt.

"Lucy's little boy. My godson," she explained, grateful for a truthful excuse not to see him. "I see his mother frequently, but I found I was so busy sometimes that I'd go for months without seeing Jeff, so I try to save Tuesdays for him. I . . . love him a lot, and I want to watch him grow up. My time with him is important to me," she added, wondering if Michael understood.

"Sort of a family night, huh?" He rather liked her loyalty to Jeff and forgave her for putting him off. He also realized he was glad she liked children, comparing her with other professional women he knew who didn't or wouldn't take the time to show it.

"I'm afraid so," she said, holding her breath for his reaction.

"Okay, Wednesday it is. Same time," he confirmed. Meghan sighed. Not only did he understand, but after Wednesday there were only two weeks to go before the beginning of her leave. She could last two weeks, she thought with Lucy's optimism.

• • •

Tuesday evening, long after Jeff had worn Meghan out and been shuffled off to bed, Meghan and Lucy sat talking and drinking steaming cups of black coffee.

"Well, you have to give him credit, Meghan. The man is no schlemiel. He's smart and clever. If you trip yourself up in one of your fibs, he's going to take you to the cleaners."

"I know, and I'm trying to be careful, but when he's around, or I talk to him on the phone, I get so nervous I can hardly think. And when he's not around, it keeps going around in my head how wonderfully . . . wonderful he is and what I've done to him," Meghan confided guiltily.

"What are you going to do if he asks you point blank about that night at the Essex," Lucy asked, pushing a plate of cookies closer to Meghan.

Meghan blew a long sigh out between pursed lips. Taking a normally forbidden cookie, she sighed once more before finally saying, "I don't know. Three-fourths of me wants to tell him the truth. He deserves it. And I know it would make me feel better. But there's still a small part of me that is too ashamed, for one thing. For another, I'm scared to death of what he'll do."

"He wouldn't hurt you?" Lucy questioned.

"No." Meghan was sure of that. "But he would definitely interfere, although I wouldn't blame him at all if he had me arrested and sent to prison for life for setting him up like I did," Meghan concluded gloomily.

"Well, you can't start getting all . . . schmaltzy at this stage. You'll think of something. You're too close to an end," Lucy tried to encourage her.

Meghan frowned at Lucy and studied her with concern. "We have to get you out of Hoboken. Have you listened to yourself talk lately? Schmaltzy, indeed!" Meghan said indignantly, before she burst into giggles.

For her date with Michael, Meghan wore a white crepe

sheath. It had two swags of loose fabric that crossed the front to conceal her burgeoning figure, a V neckline in front and back, and glittering rhinestones trimming the shoulders and long, slender sleeves. She was very pleased with this disguise. She looked anything but pregnant.

This time while she awaited Michael's arrival, there was no nausea. Try as she might, she just couldn't conjure it up. However, her ultra-healthy dose of fear was alive and thriving, she noted. She looked around the room one last time to make sure all was in order.

Clean. Tidy. Scotch and glasses out. Coat. Purse. Three-way bulbs in the lamps on high.

When the bell chimed, she opened the door to a triumphantly grinning Michael.

"You look extremely . . . healthy tonight," he said, his gaze devouring her with relish. Lord, she was beautiful.

Meghan gave a soft, embarrassed laugh and thanked him, then added, "Would you like to come in for a drink? The scotch is out," she informed him pointedly.

"Darlin'," he said regretfully, "I'd love to but I have in my possession a pair of the most coveted theater tickets in town. The show starts at eight-thirty, and the cab is waiting."

"Which show is it?" she asked enthusiastically, knowing one could not get too intimate at the theater.

"It's a surprise," he whispered secretively, then added in his normal voice, "Get those pretty buns in gear or we'll be late."

The broadway show was the season's crowd pleaser for which both Lucy and Meghan had been trying to get tickets for months. And it *was* a pleaser. A romantic comedy Meghan and Michael enjoyed tremendously.

Another delightful aspect to the evening was Michael. He was a considerate and charming companion. Meghan found herself talking to him almost as easily as she did to Lucy. Well . . . almost. Lucy's eyes didn't twinkle at her quite the way Michael's did, nor did Lucy ignite the same warm fires in Meghan that Michael's scent and slightest touch did. Nevertheless, despite the physical and mental tension his presence created, Meghan found herself responding to his easy, amicable manner.

At intermission, she mentioned that if she hadn't known for sure that he'd grown up amidst the tumble-weeds of Texas, she'd swear that he'd been brought up as part of New York's elite. The fact that he seemed to know so many of the "right" people and was so comfortable in their presence surprised her.

He grinned and divulged that as a youth he'd been so awkward and unsophisticated that at one point his mother had broken down and cried in hopelessness, and the next day his father drove him into Dallas and registered him in charm school. He went on to add that they wouldn't let him graduate until he was nearly twenty-eight years old because he invariably failed the teacup-on-the-knee test.

He said that between charm school, football practice, high school, and dance class, he was a very busy teenager.

After Meghan obligingly walked into his trap, he said that all the pretty girls in Dallas had gotten together and decided that they'd much rather chip in to pay for some dancing lessons for him than have to wear ortho-pedic shoes for the rest of their lives.

Meghan's contribution to the conversation was the humiliating fact that being nearly a foot taller than most of the boys she knew in high school, she had had to go to her senior prom on her knees.

And so the evening went. Between all the exagger-ated anecdotes of their pasts, the play, and bits and pieces of Michael's real-life history, Meghan was com-pletely captivated.

By the time they reached a cozy French restaurant on East 52nd Street, it was nearly eleven. After four months of eating at regular intervals, Meghan's stomach was now protesting angrily. It burned furiously and played nasty little tricks on her mind. When at last Meghan was handed a menu, she was sure her stomach had deserted her and left in its place a tremendous cavern.

She ordered enough food to keep herself alive for another week. The first half she ate feverishly, then she tapered off enough to join Michael in dinner conversation.

"Do you always eat like that?" Michael asked, amusement dancing in his eyes.

"Well, no," she admitted sheepishly. "It's just that I had an early lunch today, and we didn't get here until late. I'm just very hungry," she explained, then added, "If I'd known about your surprise, I'd have had a snack earlier."

"Half a side of beef?" Michael guessed.

She gave him a sassy smirk. "Don't be silly. I probably would have eaten only a couple of bananas and a watermelon."

They laughed heartily. Still smiling at her, he pronounced, "Mary Meghan Shay, you're a nice person. I like you."

Their gazes met and held. They studied each other intently, one with thrilled amazement at the man she'd thought would never walk into her life, the other plagued with questions about the woman who haunted his mind and soul, and set his emotions on fire.

With a quizzical frown and narrowed eyes, Michael tilted his head slightly to one side and quietly asked, "What the hell were you doing that night?"

Meghan's constant companions, humiliation and remorse, were there in her eyes as Michael watched her. And she knew she had earned what was coming.

She laid her fork and knife down on her plate and placed both of her trembling hands in her lap. At least her body responded when she begged it to close out the confusion and regret in Michael's eyes. Her eyes lowered to look at her hands as she waited for him to speak again.

With infinite gentleness he went on, "I don't want to hurt you, darlin', I'm just trying to understand. I most certainly don't regret that it happened, but I need to know why it did."

He sighed with frustration and restlessly ran a hand through his hair, then decided to start at the beginning.

"When I first woke up and there wasn't even the slightest trace that you'd been there, I thought maybe you'd been a fantastic dream. But bits and pieces came back to me to convince me you were real.

"When you hadn't returned by the time I had to leave for Texas, I decided that you were just some sort of frustrated woman who got her kicks seducing men in bars.

"For weeks I roamed around Dallas thinking about you. I couldn't get you off my mind. It was like something astronomical had occurred in my life, and I didn't even know what it was or why it happened. It drove me crazy. I sounded out my brother and my friends thinking they might have hired you as a lark. I even started checking the mail for blackmail pictures," he said, the exasperation still alive in his voice.

"Hiring the investigator was a spur-of-the-moment idea that came to me while I was talking to Henry about representing me in the Dobson purchase. When I decided to put Macklin on what I thought was your trail, I wasn't even sure I wanted to see you again. I just had this panicky feeling that I had to at least know you were all right, that nothing had happened to you, that you were doing whatever you did normally. It was like an obsession." He laughed wryly and told her, "It boggles my mind to think that all the time you were sitting right down the hall from Henry Alderman."

Meghan said nothing. What could she say? That she systematically picked him out of a crowd, seduced him, and made him the father of her baby without his consent?

"What was it? A practical joke? An experiment? Some sort of test?" he asked softly without anger or malice in his voice. "I suspect the night served some purpose, because I have the distinct impression that it's not something you'd do under normal circumstances."

Meghan's head came up. She quizzed him with her eyes. She appreciated the fact that he didn't think she was a crazed nymphomaniac. But if she told him the truth, he would think even worse of her. He'd never understand how much she wanted her baby. She couldn't begin to describe the burning need she felt.

Meghan's greatest problem in having expressive eyes was that they told everything she was thinking, good or bad. Michael could see her struggling with her emotions, but it was hard to see past the barriers she had erected between the two of them. He wanted desperately to help. She had some powerful force compelling her to keep quiet when it was obvious to him that she wanted to tell all. She looked so despondent and miserable.

"Tell me, Meghan," he murmured softly.

"I wish I could, Michael. I wish it had been a joke or a test or something I could explain. But I have no excuse for what I did," she said sincerely. At least half-truths were better than lies . . . or the whole truth. "All I can do is call it a really rotten thing to have done to you and beg your forgiveness."

He leaned back in his chair and examined her closely. She was still hiding the real reason, and he had a sinking feeling that she'd take it to her grave, but he couldn't resist one last try.

"You mean you saw me sitting there and you just suddenly went crazy and decided to have a night of wild, passionate sex with me?" he asked disbelievingly.

She mulled his question over for a second, then nodded. "In a way it was like that," she said honestly. "I'm sorry, but I don't regret what happened that night, only that you got so involved. I need you to believe I didn't set out to hurt you or make you worry. I just assumed you'd enjoy yourself and leave town and not give it another thought. I . . . I'll never be able to compensate you for all the grief I've caused, but I am most truly sorry," she finished, as the ring of truth in her words pealed loud and clear.

Michael expelled a resigned sigh, and came forward in his seat again. He took Meghan's soft, white hand in his big brown one and was not surprised to find it trembling.

"I believe you, Meghan. I'm aware that there's more to this story than you can bring yourself to tell me, but it's okay. Maybe someday . . ." He shrugged. "Let's just go on from here, shall we?"

Meghan nodded and whispered a heartfelt "Thank you." Warm gratitude brought a low flame of life back into her eyes, but Michael could tell she was still on very shaky ground.

"So. Tell me, when did your family move from Boston to New York?" he asked, changing the subject as if they'd just been discussing the weather. He picked up his fork to resume eating and give Meghan a chance to compose herself.

His change in strategy was apparently too fast for her, because she gave him a startled look and squeaked, "What?"

"You said you grew up in Boston. You didn't come to New York with your family?" he asked.

"No. No, I didn't." She struggled to regain her calm, grateful for his sensitivity. "I came to New York fresh out of law school. My family still lives in Boston."

"What does your father do?" he asked politely.

"He owns a pub," she informed him, aware that his own father was an oil baron and wondering if it mattered to Michael that they weren't from the same social class. It had never mattered to her before.

"So you *do* know what a drink is," he teased, referring to the night of their aborted date.

"Well, I know a decent one would never be made with oyster juice." She grinned.

They finished the evening talking about their childhoods and respective brothers. Michael's brother, Kevin, was six years younger than he. When Michael had decided to set out on his own, his parents had been disappointed but encouraging. They had hoped he'd take over the family business. Luckily, Kevin showed a great interest in the company and was now his father's right-hand man and heir apparent. Michael grinned playfully as he stated how things had a way of working out for the best, and then winked at her.

Meghan told Michael about her brothers in return. The oldest was Donald. She loved him, but he teased her horribly and sometimes not too playfully. She thought maybe he was a little envious of her, of what she'd done with her life. As children, he had always been her adversary, pointing out her misdeeds to her father, then setting her up to commit more when things got too quiet. Later the relationship only changed to a more subtle degree. He had taken a perverse joy in pretending to be overly protective of her and chasing away her boyfriends.

Now, Conrad, or Connie for short, she spoke highly of. Eighteen months older than she, they were not only close in age, but in spirit. He was truly her friend and protector and most trusted counsel. When he was old enough to place himself as a buffer between her and Donald, he had done so courageously, as Donald was four years older and much bigger. Many were the consequences Connie had taken for his love of Meghan, and she was totally devoted to him.

"Actually," she began to confess, as they entered the elevator in her apartment building, "I harbored dreams of growing up and marrying Connie. And when Pop got old, we'd take him and move to California and leave Donald all alone," she finished.

"Why California?" he asked with amusement. He could almost see her as a gangly red-headed little girl, full of trouble. He pictured a real spitfire, who skulked around and plotted the destruction of the nefarious Donald.

"California was about as far as I'd gotten in my geography lessons," she said, grinning.

They walked the short distance to her door, and while she fished around in her bag for her keys, he asked, "What made you decide not to marry Connie?"

She giggled. "Well, as you know, society frowns on that sort of thing, or I might have. I had to settle for looking for his best qualities in someone else."

"And have you found many such virtuous men?" he asked, half-joking, half-serious.

"A few," she said, unlocking her door.

"And how do I fare?"

Meghan looked up into his face. She saw a hungry longing in his eyes and was thrilled by it. Her heart thumped painfully against her ribs while a current of tingling sensations shot through her.

He was a lot like Connie. He was good and kind, understanding and patient, witty, and yes, forgiving and accepting. But the feelings she had toward him were of a far more sexual nature. Remembering the feel of his arms about her and the touch of his lips on hers made her knees go suddenly weak. Leaning on her door for support, she smiled stunningly and assured him, "You fare very well."

He smirked as his arms reached out to pull her close.

"Good. Then the feelings are mutual,' he murmured as his head lowered to stamp his seal of approval on her lips.

His kiss was warm and exploring. Meghan moaned her pleasure when she realized it wasn't going to be just a good-night peck. She raised her arms, circling them around his neck and playing with the soft half curls at his nape, as she joined in enthusiastically.

Their ardor increased, consuming them both, and when at last they parted, they were both breathless and tense with desire.

"Let's go inside," Michael whispered in a hoarse drawl.

"Not tonight, Michael," she said, and in response to his sidelong look, she pleaded, "I . . . Let's do it right this time."

He studied her for several seconds. The fear was back. He wouldn't push her, not until she could trust him enough to let their relationship progress. He sighed. "Okay, darlin'. But I think you should know I feel very right about this already."

"I'm sure you do," she said with a chuckle.

"Don't get cute, Meghan. I'm only human," he said with pride.

Seven

He called her again at the office early the next day.

"How about lunch?" he offered, his voice cheerful and confident.

"Fine," she agreed, lunch sounding considerably safer than another dinner. "Where?"

"I'll come for you about one, and you can pick the place."

"Harper's is nice for lunch, but I'll have to meet you. I have an appointment with the Dobsons' lawyers this morning," she informed him. "This is such a dull business sometimes," she complained. "Especially when I get cases like yours. I make my demands, they say okay, and it's over. There's just no meat to the deal."

"You like to dicker and get down on the floor and battle it out, I take it?" He sounded amused.

"It is what redheads do best, you know."

"I'll remember that." He chuckled.

Lunch was pleasant. They talked and laughed like old friends. Meghan found she could indeed relax and enjoy his company. There was a lot about him to enjoy. He had a tranquil charm and easy wit that influenced her to let down her guard.

It wasn't until he asked to see her again in the evening, his gray eyes overly warm, overly friendly, and just a tad too assuming, that she became wary once more.

She felt like a fool not to have seen it coming. Michael thought he had his foot in her door and that things were going to progress nicely from here on. He was building plans and hopes on a future that was going to last only another ten days. Worse yet, she envied his ignorance. She would have given up everything but her baby if she could make it all right again. If she'd waited five more months, Michael would have walked into her office and they could have fallen in love under normal circumstances.

Love? Was she falling in love with Michael Ramsey? Morbidly, she wondered which would get her first— would she ultimately die of guilt or a broken heart?

"Is that dazed expression on your face a yes or a no?" Michael broke in on her unhappy thoughts.

Meghan scrutinized him for several seconds before she could answer. She took in the strength and character in his face, the trust in his eyes, and the good-natured smile on his lips. Michael thought the whole world was right side up, and Meghan abhorred the idea of telling him it wasn't.

"I'm sorry, Michael. I have a couple of big cases coming up before the holidays, and they both still need a lot of firming up," she said, knowing the work would be twice as difficult now with more than half her mind concentrating on Michael.

He tilted his head as his eyes narrowed in mock suspicion before he asked accusingly, "You're not going to start trying to avoid me again, are you? I thought we were starting over as friends."

Oh, why couldn't he have been a jerk, she wondered. Meghan sighed before flashing Michael a perfect smile.

"I really do have a lot of work to do. Could I take a rain check for a night next week?" she bargained, as much to mollify herself as him. Refusing to spend time with him was becoming as difficult as not telling him the truth.

His disappointment obvious, Michael responded with, "Okay, but could you possibly break away for a while on Saturday? I need to look for an apartment. With things the way they are in your fair city, I thought I ought to take my attorney along."

"You're staying in New York? To live?" she asked, stunned. Would this never end?

"Eventually. In a few more months I'll have things out west set up to run relatively independent of me. For years I've been interested in the operation of periodical publications. It's actually quite different from what I'm used to, and I plan to get very involved. In fact, I have a couple of ideas I'd like to try. . . ."

He went on to tell her about his plans for Dobson Publishing, but she only half listened. This nightmare just kept going from bad to awful to worse, she thought. It wasn't a matter of avoiding him whenever possible until his business here was finished and he eventually went back to Texas where he belonged. Now, she'd have to think of another way to get him out of her life permanently—and before he found out about the baby. It didn't take long for her to admit to herself that she didn't relish the idea.

In the end her mind was too boggled to come up with a decent excuse not to go apartment hunting with him, and they set a time.

Saturday morning was sunny and cold. The wind brushed a healthful rosiness into Meghan's cheeks as she followed Michael from one apartment to the next. All told, there were four to see, but Michael managed to drag it out so they saw the last one a little after eleven-thirty. Located on 70th Street near Lexington Avenue, it was roomy with lots of windows. The Hunter College campus was visible, as well as a lovely but not overly expansive view of the New York skyline.

"I like this one," Meghan said, as she opened a door to inspect the size of the closet. Not very domesticated, Meghan had asked Lucy to choose her apartment for her. She did, however, know that an apartment with lots of places to put things out of sight was desirable.

"The storage space here is wonderful," she quoted Lucy from years ago.

"I don't know. Maybe we should decide over lunch. I usually don't like making quick decisions." *Usually*, he reiterated to himself. Lately he'd made quite a few quick, easy decisions. The one that had surprised him the most was the one he'd made about Meghan. It had come quietly, peacefully, moving into his heart and soul unobtrusively and making itself at home. He was totally besieged by her; his white flag was up.

As the beauty of her face and the seduction of her body had attracted him, her perception and wit had captured him. Still, there was so much he didn't know about her—a mystery he had every intention of solving, just as he had every intention of keeping her in his life.

During the meal he pointed out several good aspects of the three previous places they'd seen, but Meghan stuck to her guns, insisting he'd be glad for the space later.

"Besides," she added convincingly, "the open spaces, all those windows, and the hardwood trim gives it so much . . . character."

"And we all know what an excellent judge of character you are," he teased.

Meghan's head flew up to find merriment dancing in his eyes. There were no accusations, no malice, only an easy, good-natured humor behind his deep chuckle.

"That's right," she said, giving her head a confident nod and Michael a cocky grin.

In the end, he chose her favorite apartment with the stipulation that when he was ready to move in, she would help him. Appealing to her nonexistent domestic nature, he reinforced his argument, saying that everyone knew how inept men were when it came to knowing the right places for sofas and pictures.

She had laughed at the irony of his request, and he took it as her assent. She didn't correct him. It hurt somehow, but she knew that once she was gone, he'd find a more knowledgeable, able-bodied woman to do the job.

Michael was grinning smugly. Not only had he known she'd like the apartment when he'd signed the lease a little over a week ago, but he had conned her into helping him decorate. His mother would be disappointed, but he'd make it up to her. Right now he needed the time. Time to see Meghan and get to know her better. She was so damned busy, it was hard getting a date with her. She did, however, seem to make time for him if he needed her, and at this point he wasn't above stooping to trumped-up excuses and a little clever manipulating.

Sunday he called her apartment, panic ringing in his voice.

"Meghan. I've got to see you one last time. My unit's been called up. They're moving us to the front lines," he told her without preamble. "This could be our last chance to see one another. I . . . I could die out there," he added grimly.

"Who is this?" She feigned indignation, then laughed, giving herself away.

"Ah! Low blow! I thought I could trust you. I thought you'd wait for me. I thought you'd burn a candle in your window for me."

"You can. I am. I will . . . along with all the others. I may have to move though. I'm running out of window space," she said in a happy voice.

A few seconds passed before Michael spoke. "You're breaking my heart," he said seriously.

"You know it's not intentional," she offered in a similar tone.

"I really am leaving tomorrow," he told her. "And I really would like to see you again before I leave." He paused briefly. "Can you spare the time?" he asked, knowing what it was like to be overworked, to have deadlines to meet. She'd already taken some time-out for him, and although he'd kill to be with her, he'd much rather have her mind at ease for her upcoming cases in court.

"Yes," Meghan informed him. Her heart was suddenly heavy and each beat sent a shaft of pain shooting through her chest.

"If I bring dinner, may I come over?" he asked, his pulse racing, his muscles tense from the need to be with her.

"Of course," she said. Stunned by her sorrow, it was hard to believe she had been anxiously awaiting this day. She bit her lip to keep from blurting out, "Don't go. When you come back, I'll be gone. You'll hate me. We'll never see each other again. Don't go!"

"Do you like the Chinese food from that little place around the corner from your apartment?" she heard him ask.

"Yes. It's good."

"Anything special you want me to get?"

"No. It's all delicious," she said, then reconsidered, "I'm not crazy about anything raw, though."

"Come on. I know you can eat more than that." He had brought enough food to feed half the Chinese population. She had eaten so hungrily every time he'd taken her out, he hadn't been sure how much to order. He liked women who didn't pick at their food all night, but Meghan ate like a ranch hand.

"No. Really. I'm full. And I told you before I don't always pig out like that. It's just that I'm used to eating at certain times and if I don't, I get ravenous. If you'd stick to my schedule, I'd be a much cheaper date," she said, trying to lighten the tension that had been building steadily since he'd arrived.

"Oh, I don't mind feeding you. I'm just afraid you'll explode all over the restaurant. How could I possibly explain it to the management?"

"Michael, I'm shocked that you'd even think I'd ever do that to you. I was brought up with much better manners. Exploding in public was strictly forbidden," she retorted.

"I'm sure," he teased, "But it makes me very curious to know where you put it all."

"If all things in this world were as easy to explain as that, it would be a much simpler place to live," she prophesied.

He waited for her revelation, and when it didn't come, he finally asked, "Where *do* you put it?"

"I have a hollow leg."

Michael's eyes grew wide in mock wonderment. "How fascinating. Which one is it?"

Meghan indicated her left one and before she realized the error of her ways, he had lifted the leg and placed it across his lap. He held it out and turned it slightly from side to side. He gave it a few gentle raps with his knuckles, working his way up from ankle to mid-thigh, all the while sending waves of tingling excitement rushing through Meghan's body.

Her heart beat wildly. Her mouth was dry and she wanted to say something pithy and witty, but nothing came to mind. She was too busy absorbing the feel of his hand through her jeans and the sensations he was creating in her.

"This is incredible, Meghan," he said softly in awe. "A work of art. It looks perfectly natural. No hollow sound," he continued, as he began to push her pant leg up, his hands touching her bare skin, intensifying her susceptibility a hundredfold. "And look at this," he crowed. "Completely impervious to light. Opaque. Beautiful. They could use you in espionage work."

He rubbed his hands lightly over her calf and re-garded her with interest. "Do you have any other secret hiding places? Your arm, maybe?" He drew his hand down the length of her left arm, adding a new source of stimulation to Meghan's already overexcited body.

She shook her head negatively in answer to his question.

"No? Maybe your head then?" he asked, as he placed both big hands on either side of her face.

Again she shook her head. She felt mesmerized, com-pletely under his spell. She was powerless to stop him. "Now you're lying to yourself," she thought to herself hopelessly. "You could stop him if you wanted to. You just don't want to. You want to make love with him one last time. You want him because you're falling in love with him."

Meghan's most precious wish lay exposed in her eyes. Michael's heart soared and his body quickened. He struggled for control as he said, "Are you sure? When you shake your head like that I hear a distinct rattle."

He pressed his lips gently, sensuously to hers. He savored the taste and feel of her. As his fever grew, he explored with his tongue, memorizing her softness, the sweetness that was Meghan's alone.

Meghan returned his kisses and did some research of her own. Their passion intensified as they became bolder and more possessive. Their hands caressed and petted, each feeding the fires in the other.

Michael's drawl was raspy and hoarse when he mur-mured between soft kisses along the column of her neck. "This time we will do it right. We'll make love all night long and into tomorrow. I'm not going to let you disappear on me again. And I'll warn you now, I don't plan to be easily forgotten while I'm gone."

"Oh, Michael." She moaned. There was no way she could ever forget him. She would disappear again . . . and he'd hate her forever. But they did have tonight.

He stood and held out a hand to her. She took it, and

he drew her into his embrace. "This has got to go," he said, as he tugged on the rear tail of her oversized sweatshirt.

"You don't like it?" she asked him innocently. "Is it too provocative?"

He leaned back, frowning, and viewed the front of her shirt, which sported the words, "WHEN GOD CREATED MAN, SHE WAS ONLY JOKING." He slipped his hands underneath the material and ran them over her back. "As I recall, what is under this provokes far less hostile thoughts," he said with a lecherous grin.

"Well, if you can't take a joke, let's by all means remove the offending piece of clothing."

"By all means . . . let's," he purred, as he took the hem of her shirt in his large hands and pulled it up her body and over her head.

Her loose hair fell forward on her shoulders and partially veiled her bare breasts from his sight. She'd worn denim slacks with an elastic waistband for comfort, but Michael found it a great convenience as he simply slid them off her hips and to the floor, leaving only her navy blue bikini panties behind.

He committed her body to memory with reverent eyes. One hand came out to play with the downy-soft tress of red hair that fell over her left breast, and then he gathered up the strands, letting the back of his hand brush across her hardened nipple before he placed the fall of hair behind her.

He viewed her once more, then leaned forward and kissed her deeply. "Meghan," he said with a groan, as he held her tight against his rock hard chest. "I want you so much."

"And I want you," she murmured against his throat, as she kissed and gently nibbled at his skin.

They turned slowly toward the bedroom, touching and kissing and whispering words of love to each other.

"No ride this time?" she asked as she luxuriated in the feel of him so close to her.

"I wouldn't want to risk it. I can hardly walk as it is."

They laughed softly, intimately together. Moments later they were both naked and lying on the bed, Meghan on her back running her fingers through the coarse, dark hair on his chest, Michael with his head propped on one elbow as he moved the other hand slowly over her skin from her neck to her pelvis.

"You are so beautiful. More so than I remembered," he told her.

"Only because you think I am. Then I feel like I am, which makes you think I am. It's a lovely cycle, isn't it?" she murmured, as she moved her head slightly to kiss his chin.

"Mmm. Lovely," he repeated in his thick, deep voice, as he lowered his lips to hers.

Their loving was long and leisurely, the crescendo building gradually to a fevered cadenza and finally an explosive finale.

They clung together, warm and content. They whispered and giggled in the dark. They dozed for a while, and then woke with a hunger only the other could vanquish.

Meghan lay awake, listening to Michael breathe as she watched the dawn slowly illuminate the room. Slowly, careful not to wake him, she tilted her head up to look at him.

His eyes were closed and his long lashes fanned out across his cheeks, but he was smiling. "That was very good. I don't think I've ever seen you motionless for so long," came his deep voice, gravelly from sleep. He peeked at her with one eye, then tightened his embrace to cuddle closer.

"I just kept hoping that if I didn't move, time would stand still and this wouldn't end," she said, as she molded her body closer to his.

"I know," he murmured, squirming to get even closer to her. "But this isn't the end, it's only the beginning."

"Lord, what a cuddly person you are." She cheerfully

and affectionately changed the subject. "You're like a big, lovable teddy bear."

"Then I'm glad to see you like teddy bears," he said.

"What makes you think I do?" She chuckled as he shifted positions again.

"Is that or is that not a teddy bear?" he asked, as he rolled over and pointed to the soft, brown toy on Meghan's dresser.

She had forgotten about it completely. The teddy bear with its big red ribbon had been too tempting when she'd seen it in the store window yesterday. She'd gone in and picked it up, testing its softness. She had known instantly that her baby had to have it. When she'd gotten home, she'd propped him lovingly on her dresser. He was there to help her wait for the arrival of their baby.

"That's for a friend of mine," she said hastily.

"A young one, I hope," he said, grinning.

"Oh, I expect when I meet him, he'll be very, very young," she whispered whimsically, almost to herself.

"A friend of yours is having a baby?" he inquired offhandedly, as he smoothed his hand over her barely rounded abdomen. He pictured her carrying his baby and warmed to the idea immediately.

"Yes, she's very close to me," Meghan replied as honestly as she thought she could without causing him heart failure.

"That's wonderful," he murmured against her neck, aware of the reawakening desire inside him. "I like children."

"So do I," she whispered, as his lips came up to press tenderly on hers.

Eight

Meghan could vaguely remember her mother's funeral. She had cried without really knowing why, but was aware that part of her life was missing and nothing would ever be the same. She wanted to cry this morning for the same reasons, plus the added grief of knowing why.

"Lord, I hate that look on your face, darlin', but it makes me so happy," Michael said, planting another kiss on her mouth as they said their good-byes in front of her apartment building. "Cheer up, Meghan, love, the month will fly by, and we'll be together again." He kissed her long and hard once more, then raced off to his cab, calling, "I'll phone you tonight."

Meghan only nodded, not trusting herself to open her mouth. He called her from the airport, not waiting until he'd reached Dallas, and caught her at the office on her way out to have lunch with a client.

"Hi." His voice came cheerfully over the line. Meghan had just accustomed herself to the sluggish, depressed feeling that had prevailed throughout her morning, only to have her heart skip a beat and begin a rapid tapping at the mere sound of his voice.

"Hi," she returned breathlessly. "Where are you?"

"I'm still at Kennedy. My plane was delayed so I thought I'd give you a second chance to try and entice me into staying in New York. I'm feeling very susceptible to emotional blackmail right now," he hinted.

"I thought this was an important trip," she returned thoughtfully, as a satisfied smile played unconsciously at her lips.

"It is, or I wouldn't be going right now, but I still wouldn't object to you making a fuss and maybe whining and crying a little," he said.

"That's not exactly my style," she returned, unable to suppress the giggle at the back of her throat.

"So I've noticed," he informed her bluntly. "Would you consider packing a bag and going with me if I took a later flight out of here?"

"Well," she said, "that is more my style, but the timing is all wrong."

Playful banter could be addictive with Michael around. She loved his wit and intelligence, but they were only one part of what she was going to miss about him. On that thought her spirits came crashing back to earth and, more resolute than ever, she sat up straighter in her chair.

"We both have busy professional lives," she reminded him. "That makes . . . other things a little complicated, doesn't it?"

"In this case, the . . . other things are well worth making time for, Meghan. And I may as well warn you, darlin', if I feel you slipping away from me again, there won't be anything in Texas important enough to keep me from coming back," he told her firmly. And she believed him.

He called that night, and every morning and night after that, right up until the time Meghan had to leave town. As he had predicted, the time had flown by.

Instead of the usual slow work period at the office during the holidays, things picked up after Thanksgiving. Two of Meghan's cases came to trial earlier than expected, and her appointments in the office were arranged back-to-back.

Her busy schedule, the fatigue of her pregnancy, and the anguish she felt over Michael began to show. She lost weight, which Lucy chastised her for severely and called Mrs. Belinski with a special high protein, high calorie diet and charged her with the duty of making sure Meghan ate it.

She didn't look much better a week later when she entered Henry Alderman's office.

"I've finished the Ramsey case. Do you want it? All we need is his signature and his check. The papers to incorporate Dobsons' into Texacal are in the file too. He just has to sign them," she finished.

"Sure. It'll be a good excuse to see him again," he said. Henry gave her a speculative look, then asked, "What did you think of him?"

Meghan shrugged noncommittally. "He's okay. Why?"

"When I met him, I was very curious about the effect he would have on a red-blooded woman . . . such as yourself," he explained, as his lips twitched to keep himself from grinning. Henry's grin became hard to conceal as he watched her squirm in her chair, a slight rosiness flushing her cheeks.

Discussing Michael Ramsey as a client was part of her job and he was a topic that she had to handle professionally, but discussing him as a man was disturbing to her. She cleared her throat gently, then replied, "He's just another client, Henry, and you know I don't get involved with clients."

"I see," he said with a straight face, as he looked down at the paperwork before him. "So, when is this client supposed to come sign these papers?"

"I'm not sure. I have to call him about a couple of small matters, so I'll let him know that he is to contact you when he gets back," she said, preparing to go. "I'll leave my files and summaries with your secretary before

I go, and you can dole them out. And Greta knows how to reach me if the need arises."

"We'll muddle through somehow, Meghan," Henry told her, letting her know that no one was indispensable. "You look like hell. Every time I see you I'm afraid you'll drop dead at my feet," he said unmercifully. "Enjoy yourself, Meghan. I'll miss you. Even anemic and exhausted, you're one of the best attorneys, not to mention people, I know."

"All right Henry. Thank you," she said with mixed emotions. She hated leaving her partners in a bind, but she was mentally, emotionally, and physically drained . . . and her precious secret would be showing soon. Besides, maybe if she had some time alone and some rest, she could sort out her feelings about Michael.

"Henry, if I don't see you, Merry Christmas." She smiled at him fondly and let herself out of his office.

That night Meghan sat alone in her darkened apartment, the phone settled in her lap and clutched tightly in both hands. It was her last night in town, her last chance to talk to Michael, the time to tell him about the baby.

It hadn't been an easy decision to make, but her love for Michael and her guilt had won out over her shame and selfishness. She would tell him about the baby. Either way, she'd never be able to have Michael himself. They just weren't ever meant to be. She at least could try her best to do what was right in regard to visitation and . . .

"Oh, Michael. I wish that you could know how much I love you, how much I wish things were different," she cried, her lungs tight, every beat of her heart causing an excruciating pain. But he couldn't, and they weren't, and she owed him the truth.

Michael was a good, honest man. A man of strong character, he would be hurt and outraged beyond belief if he ever discovered the truth from anyone but her. Because she loved him, she was willing to allow him to hate her. She'd tell him about their baby.

Her sobs abating, she prepared herself to sound calm and endure an inferno as she dialed the phone.

"Everything is all set. All you need to do is bring your money and sign your name," she told him after the routine "How are you's." Then she cheerfully added, "However . . . the Dobson brothers have decided they would like to put out a Fortieth Anniversary issue late this summer. They said we could go ahead with the deal, and you could move in anytime, but they would like complete control and ownership until after the anniversary issue." She paused briefly. "Knowing how you feel about those two, I said I couldn't see any problem, but that I'd have to check with you first to make sure. However," she added again hastily, "I went ahead and drew up the final papers with that stipulation included. I'm too busy to rewrite them, so don't disappoint me and suddenly turn greedy," she teased.

"I would have been disappointed in you if you had thought I wouldn't okay it," he said. Actually, it was wonderful, he thought. With everything tied up in the west and with light getting-to-know-the-ropes duties at Dobson, he'd have plenty of time to spend with Meghan.

These last two weeks had been frustrating and miserable for him. He thought about her constantly. He relived every moment he'd spent with her, remembering every word she had said and the way she had laughed. He pictured her tossing that mane of hair over her shoulders and their last night together.

She still harbored a secret she couldn't bring herself to tell him, but he knew she would trust him in time. She was warm, intelligent, witty, and exceptionally beautiful, and he loved her. He needed and wanted her in his life. He planned to find a way to make her trust and love and need him in return. He had to find a way. He was falling hard and he knew it, and, while the last two weeks had been frustrating and miserable, he had never been happier or more optimistic in his life.

He asked about work and she told him of two cases coming to court earlier than predicted, her heavy work load, and how she was so exhausted, she practically crawled off to bed every night. She said she'd been going into the office early and staying late, just to get everything done before the holidays. As she was planning to visit her family in Boston, she didn't want a ton of work hanging over her head the whole time.

"I probably won't be able to get back until after the first of the year. This little problem shouldn't take too much time, but as long as I'm here, I'll finish up a few other things. Then I won't need to come back to Texas until the end of the summer," he explained, obviously expecting her to be in New York when he got back.

Now was the time. She couldn't put off telling him her secret any longer.

"Michael," she started tentatively, then drew a long breath and released it. "Michael, I . . ." She sighed deeply again, unable to get enough air. "I have something I need to tell you . . . something important." She paused, again gulping for air.

"Everything you say to me is important," he said intimately. "By the way, have I told you yet how crazy I am about you?"

Meghan's response was silence. Her nerve was gone. His words had destroyed her good intentions and at the same time had torn her heart into a million tortured pieces.

"Meghan? Are you there?" a worried Michael broke in.

"Yes."

"I'm listening. What was it you wanted to tell me?" he asked, his voice still conveying his concern.

"I . . ." She couldn't do it. "I left your file with Henry. So if you get back to town before I do and want to wrap things up, he can help you."

"Okay. Was that all?" he questioned, sensing there was more she wanted to say.

"Yes . . . no . . . I miss you, Michael," fell from her mouth before she could stop it.

"Oh, Meghan, darlin'. I miss you too. More than I can say," he almost purred with happiness. "I'd give anything to be there with you, to hold you again." He paused thoughtfully, then added, "Look, I'm going to try and hustle things along here. Maybe I can get back before you leave town for the holidays."

"No, Michael," she said in a rush, "I mean, go ahead and finish it all up. Spend the holidays with your own family and . . . well, there's no sense in having to go back right away if you can take care of it all now while you're there," she said, hoping she sounded logical.

"I guess," Michael conceded reluctantly. "But I'm dying to be with you again."

"I know," she said softly, empathizing with him.

A week later Meghan was in New Bedford at her Aunt Kate's, where she planned to stay until after she had the baby. The lovely old woman had welcomed her with open arms, congratulating her on her pregnancy, and told her how wonderful it was that Meghan was going to pass on the Shay red hair.

Aunt Kate was Meghan's father's aunt and nearly eighty—but most of the time it was hard to tell. She was definitely a pixy, a sweet, kind soul who rode a bicycle everywhere she went and dyed her once "Shay red hair" red, which managed to turn it a peculiar shade of orange.

In Meghan's desolate frame of mind, Aunt Kate was a true godsend. She made Meghan feel welcome and loved, and best of all, she made her laugh.

"Meghan, dear, where are you?" Kate greeted from the kitchen door. It was late afternoon on the day before Christmas Eve.

Meghan had lain down for a short nap that had extended to two hours. Groggy, she called out to her aunt.

"Oh, sweetheart," Kate exclaimed as she bustled into the room. "I've just received the most terrible news. Freddy Preston fell on his front stoop and broke his hip a week ago, and I simply must go. You'll be fine here alone, won't you? I mean, we do have a little time before your baby comes, don't we?" she asked anxiously.

"Yes. Of course. Plenty of time. Four more months, but . . ."

"Well, it shouldn't take me that long to get Freddy back on his hip," interrupted Aunt Kate. "He's such a marvelous dancer. This is such a shame, but he really is one of my favorites, and I feel I ought to be with him. You understand, don't you, dear?"

"Certainly, but Aunt Kate, who is Freddy?" Meghan asked, not understanding it all.

"Freddy Preston is one of my most favorite beaux. We've been courting for years," the older woman explained, a dreamy expression on her face.

"Oh? How many?" Meghan asked, as she bit into her cheeks to keep from grinning.

"Well, let me see," the orange-haired lady pondered. "I met Freddy just after my birthday that year . . . yes, it was the year I turned fifty-six. How many years is that?" she asked, as she raised her fingers and began to count rapidly.

"Quite a few." Meghan chuckled. "He believes in long courtships, doesn't he?"

"Not Freddy," Kate replied with disgust. "He's constantly after me to marry him."

"He is? Don't you love him?" she asked, enjoying the conversation.

"I do love him, but I also love my other beaux. It's just that after Stewart died, bless his soul, I found that certain pleasures in life are more enjoyable and far more exciting if you change partners occasionally. The spice of life, you know."

"I always thought practice makes perfect," Meghan said, thinking her aunt meant dancing and bridge partners. "But I suppose it could get dull after a while."

"Oh, sex is never boring, dear." Her aunt gave her an amazed look. "But there is good sex, much better sex, and truly exciting sex. I just . . ."

"You mean . . ." Meghan interrupted, astonished.

Her aunt gave her an indulgent smile and a sassy wink. "I may be old, dear, but I'm not dead, and love keeps my spirit young."

Meghan couldn't argue with that. She only wished she could say the same about her love. Instead she was lonely, miserable, and feeling very old.

Sitting alone over her congealing TV dinner on Christmas Eve, Meghan called Lucy at her parents' home using the pretext of wanting to wish them all a Merry Christmas. In actuality, she merely wanted to hear some friendly voices.

"He's still calling your apartment," Lucy informed her. Lucy had been to Meghan's apartment to check on the mail and to listen for any important phone messages. Mrs. Belinski had agreed to come in once a week to dust and to water the plants. Meghan, knowing a gem when she saw one, and not wanting to lose her, had insisted on paying Mrs. Belinski full wages until she returned home with the baby.

"Couldn't you call him? Maybe try to explain things? He sounds so desperate to talk to you, but he's being very patient. I believe he thinks you're terribly busy at work. He just asks 'Would you please call me when you get a couple of seconds?' Meghan, he's breaking my heart," Lucy told her, obviously sympathizing with Michael.

"Lucy, what can I do? This is painful for me, too, you

know. And it won't hurt him as bad or for as long as the truth would," she tried to explain, knowing she was wrong.

"I suppose not," Lucy conceded. "I feel awful for him, though. For both of you, actually." She asked about Meghan's health and how well she was eating, and, of course, about Aunt Kate's latest antics. Then she added, "Guess what Mrs. Belinski is doing?"

"What?"

"She's putting up your wallpaper! She says she feels 'di guilt' taking your money and doing nothing for it, so she's fixing up the nursery. She went out and brought the cutest material for curtains, and she's nearly finished papering one wall already."

"What a nice lady. I'll think of something nice to do for her in return," Meghan said, feeling awful that people were being so nice to her, and all she seemed able to do was to cause them pain.

"I think she's enjoying it," Lucy was saying. " 'Di,' little ducks are so sweet," she mimicked the Polish woman's accent.

Lucy prattled on about her parents and Jeff's excitement, but Meghan was only half listening. Her mind wandered to thoughts of Texas and Michael, who was innocently sitting there, trusting that she'd call him, assuming that they had a future together, ignorant of the fact that he'd fathered a child.

By the time she had wished Lucy and her family a Merry Christmas and finally ended the conversation, Meghan was so filled with regret that she was nauseous. Quickly, before the feeling could hide itself in her fear again, she scrambled about in her purse for Michael's phone number.

When an unfamiliar male answered his phone in Dallas, she felt herself falter briefly before finally asking for Michael. From the sounds in the background, she guessed he was having a party, not a great time to tell someone he was about to become a father—especially under the circumstances—but it was now or never.

"May I ask who is calling, please?" the man asked politely.

"Meghan Shay," she replied.

The man laughed. "Thank God! I guess Christmas can go on as scheduled now. He's been impossible to live with lately. This call will cheer him up, thank you very much," he said merrily. "By the way, I'm his brother, Kevin, and I'm dying to meet you. It takes a lot to get my brother steamed up about anything, much less a woman who doesn't return his calls. I tend to fall in love on an average of about twice a week, but this is a first for ol' Mike, and I don't mind telling you, I've been enjoying it tremendously. Hold on now. Don't hang up. He'll want to take this on another line so it'll be a couple of seconds," he said in one breath before Meghan could get a word in edgewise.

That Michael had been talking about her to his family only darkened the gloom closing in on her. She steeled herself and wondered what she was going to say while she waited for Michael to answer.

When he finally did, he was breathless and obviously excited. "Oh, Lord, Meghan, talk to me," he exclaimed without preamble. "I just want to hear your voice . . . wait a minute, darlin' . . . Dammit, Kevin, hang up!" he ordered. There was a fraternal laugh and a click on the line.

"Sounds like I called at a bad time," Meghan noted for lack of something better to say.

"There's no such thing as a bad time for one of your calls," he said, his voice still agitated. "Are you all right? I've been worried sick."

Now or never, now or never, now or never, she told herself over and over again. "Don't be," she finally said, her voice harsh from the strain. "Don't worry about me, don't be crazy about me, don't do anything but be quiet and listen to me."

"Meghan," he started, confused and still concerned.

"Listen, Michael. I have to tell you this now or I never will. Just be quiet for a minute and let me say it. Please," she pleaded, her tone desperate.

"Sure, darlin'," he said softly, fear and tension evident in his voice. He had a feeling she was about to say good-bye.

There was silence between them as Meghan forced herself to breathe in and out. She suddenly had an overwhelming craving for a cigarette, and she'd never smoked in her life.

Slowly, she started. "I know it's a coward's way of doing this, I should tell you face to face . . . and I couldn't have picked a worse time to do it, but I . . . well, it's not going to be easy to say, and I have the courage now so . . ." She trailed off, realizing she wasn't making much sense.

Taking yet another deep breath, she started over, "Michael, I want to tell you something . . ."

"I'm listening," he confirmed, as he recognized the words from their last conversation. This must be what she had meant to tell him then, he decided, still waiting for the gut punch.

"One day, very soon, I'm going to have your child," she stated bravely, but dying a thousand deaths.

Michael laughed in relief, then replied in a seductive drawl, "That's the way I like to hear you thinking, darlin'; I'm rather fond of the idea myself and can't wait to get started. Tell me," he started to ask, feeling restored and very amused, "would you like to get married first or just jump right into this?"

"Dammit, Michael. Listen to me," Meghan shouted over the line, exasperated beyond belief at having to tell him a second time. "I'm going to have your baby . . . soon . . . I'm already pregnant."

Silence.

"Michael?" Meghan called softly, hesitantly.

"Where are you?" he asked calmly.

"Why do you want to know?" she returned suspiciously.

"Because we can't get married over the phone," he explained.

"We can't get married, period," she stated firmly.

"Think again," he instructed, even more firmly.

"Michael," she said, falling back into her attorney's voice, "I refuse to marry you. When I get back to New York, after the baby is born, I promise I'll call you. You can see the baby whenever you want. When it's older, you can even take it to Texas . . . for a visit, if you want to. I . . . I'm sorry I did this to you," she said, her professional tone cracking around the edges. "Although I'm not sorry about the baby. I've wanted this baby forever," she finished, but added to herself, *I want it even more now, because it's yours, Michael.*

"Meghan," a still oddly relaxed Michael started to say.

"No," Meghan cut him off. "I can't discuss this anymore, Michael," she said, the tears rolling down her cheeks. "I'll call you in a few months, and we'll talk it over then . . . I'm so sorry."

The line went dead.

In the time it took Michael to hang up the phone, he'd already acknowledged that even though he was somewhat stunned by the news, he was deliriously happy. He was in love with Meghan, and she was pregnant with his child. What could be better? They could be married, he answered silently.

Michael didn't even try to delude himself about the problems he was facing. Meghan was going to resist marriage on some stupid principle or another unless he could convince her otherwise. Lord, he could have kicked himself for not telling her he loved her before leaving New York. But he'd opted for a courtship to give Meghan time to come around. If he'd told her, she'd know he wanted to marry her for herself and not just because of the infant. Now he'd have to cover twice the territory in half the time.

First things first, he thought to himself, rubbing his hands together determinedly. First he had to find out where she was.

After she hung up the phone, a deathly silence filled the house. Meghan looked around her. Not very Christmassy, she thought. The snow was nice, but the aluminum tree left a lot to be desired. She contemplated the small pile of gifts from family and friends, but decided to open them when she was less depressed. She had a feeling Santa Claus wouldn't even stop to see her this year. She hadn't been on her best behavior lately.

Wallowing in self-pity, she turned out the lights and went to bed early.

Nine

Less than forty-eight hours later Michael was back in New York. The day after Christmas was crazy in Manhattan with people returning gifts and shopping for sales. Not sure if the office would be open, he opted to go to her apartment first, praying that being newly pregnant, she had decided to stay home rather than face a visit with her family.

He arrived in time to find a woman in her late fifties, her head wrapped with a scarf and her heavy winter overcoat bound tightly against the cold, letting herself out of Meghan's apartment.

"Hello," he greeted her, pleased that Meghan was home and this woman was leaving, so they could be alone. He stepped up to the door and pressed the bell, grinning.

The woman watched him with a suspicious eye. After he rang the bell a second time, she finally said, "What you think you do? Ms. Shay not here."

"Then what were you doing in there?" he countered, just as wary.

"I check di little fuzzy ducks," she stated with dignity, her arms crossed over her bosom, daring him to top her motive for being there.

"Fuzzy ducks?" he asked, feeling as if he had suddenly walked into the Twilight Zone.

"The fuzzy ducks on di wall. I put up yesterday. I make sure they stick," she explained simply.

Eerie music began to play in the back of his mind. "I . . . see. And who are you?" he asked the alien.

"Mrs. Belinski, di housekeeper," she said. "And you?"

"I'm Michael Ramsey. A good friend of Meghan's," he added, hoping it might carry some influence. "Can you tell me where she is?"

"No. I talk to Lucy, she talks to Ms. Shay."

"Lucy?" There was that name again. Meghan had stated, "Lucy says," "Lucy thinks," at least fifty times. Why hadn't he asked about her? Who the hell was this Lucy?

"Yah. She takes di mail and phone calls for Ms. Shay," Mrs. Belinski explained.

"Oh. Well, thank you. If you do see her soon, would you tell her I stopped by," he said. So Lucy was her secretary, he thought. Who would know better where to find Meghan?

Now he knew definitely that she was out of town. Assuming Meghan had gone to her father's for Christmas, he'd need an address. He couldn't recall that she had ever mentioned the name of her father's bar in Boston, and he'd already counted a hundred and sixty-eight Shays in the Boston phone book. Calling them all would keep him busy for days, not to mention that it was impractical and highly embarrassing.

Therefore her office would be next on Michael's list. Thank God for Henry. He'd know where Meghan was.

Acting on a disgruntling hunch, he stopped in the lobby of Meghan's apartment building and phoned the office. He got a recorded message that confirmed his worst assumption. The office was closed for a long weekend. He could leave his number and name, and they'd return his call Monday.

By Monday morning he was not only angry at the

setback, he was restless from the frustration of having wasted time. It was just like before, with Meghan uppermost in his mind and him unable to find her.

"Alderman, Darkwell and Gibbs," came the answering receptionist.

"This is Michael Ramsey. May I speak to Lucy, Meghan Shay's secretary, please?" he asked tersely.

"I'm sorry, sir. Her secretary's name is Greta, and she is out of the office," her whiny voice informed him.

"Then let me talk to Henry Alderman," he said, exasperated.

"Mr. Alderman is in court today and isn't expected back in the office until tomorrow. Can I have him call you then?" she asked politely.

"No. Tell him I'll be in to see him," he answered, regretting the cutting edge in his voice. It wasn't the receptionist's fault he'd be cooling his heels for another day.

The next day Henry arrived at the office to find Michael Ramsey in the reception area, waiting to pounce on him.

"Michael. Good to see you. Meghan said you wouldn't be back until after the New Year," Henry greeted him jovially.

"Where is she, Henry?" Michael asked without preamble.

"Come into my office. I presume you're talking about Meghan?" he inquired.

"Yes, of course it's Meghan."

"Well if it's those contracts you're worried about, she turned them all over to me. You can sign them now if you'd like," Henry said, instinctively knowing it wasn't what Michael wanted to hear. "This visit is about business, isn't it?"

"Well, no . . . it's personal," he said, reluctant to

endanger Meghan's professional integrity, but desperate to find her.

"I see," said Henry with a pleased and knowing smile.

"No, I don't think you do. I was having her do some personal legal work for . . ." he broke off as he watched Henry's smile turn to a skeptical grin. "Okay. So you've got great eyesight," he conceded. "Where the hell is she?"

"She's gone," he stated simply, holding out for more information.

"Don't start with me, Henry. I'm at the end of my rope," he snarled through his teeth, showing a supreme effort to control his temper.

"You do have a time keeping track of women, don't you?" Henry pushed on fearlessly.

"Henry," he said in a deadly tone.

"She's on sabbatical for a year," he informed the despairing man.

"A year!" Michael roared, stunned. "When did she leave?"

"Two weeks ago."

"Do you know where she went?" he asked hopefully.

"No. But I do know why she needed some time off," Henry offered. To Michael's surprised look, he said, "She's been ill lately. Anemic, run-down, and overworked. She's planning on six months to get fit again and then possibly doing some volunteer legal work. She just needed a rest, and she deserves one."

Meghan obviously hadn't made a public announcement about the baby yet. As she was planning on single parenthood, Michael understood, but once they were married, he planned to hire a skywriter to publicize it.

"How can I reach her?" Michael asked flat out, leaving Henry no room to consider withholding the information from him.

Henry gave him a considering perusal anyway, then finally decided to say, "She left her whereabouts with her secretary. Since it was a short work week, Greta took it off. Would you like me to call her at home?"

"Please," Michael requested. Now that he was finally getting some cooperation, his tone of voice softened considerably.

While Henry talked to Greta, Michael restlessly paced the room. All this wasted time when he could be with Meghan convincing her that they were in love, that the baby was the best accident that would ever befall them, that the three of them should make a life together, that . . .

"I should have known," chuckled Henry, breaking into Michael's agitated thoughts. "Meghan told Greta if we needed anything to contact Lucy. Lucy knows . . ."

"Lucy knows . . . Lucy says . . ." bellowed a thwarted Michael. "What is she? A guru?"

Henry laughed aloud. "No, she's a doctor. And Meghan's closest friend. They're like sisters. One doesn't take a breath without the other one knowing."

"Well how do I reach this Lucy?" Michael challenged.

"Easy. She runs an OB clinic in Hoboken."

There were several such clinics in Hoboken. When Michael finally tracked down the appropriate one, he was informed that the enlightened Lucy had drawn holiday duty. She would be on call at the clinic from three P.M. New Year's eve until the same time New Year's Day. And, no, they weren't allowed to give out home phone numbers.

Temporarily stymied once again, he went to his apartment. None of the things had arrived from Dallas yet and the place was as empty as he felt. He wandered through the silent rooms, remembering Meghan as she'd peered into closets, checked the view from the windows and run her hands over the mahogany appreciatively.

His mind was riddled with questions. Once he found

out from Lucy where Meghan was, maybe the all-knowing Lucy could also tell him how best to proceed.

His usual bull-by-the-horns technique might not be the best approach in a situation like this or with a woman like Meghan. She might very well be feisty enough to dig in and fight him just to save her pride. Michael experienced an unreasonable and uncharacteristic pang of jealousy when he forced himself to admit Lucy probably knew a lot about Meghan that he hadn't had time to discover yet.

The next day at four, Michael walked into Lucy's clinic. The waiting room was unusually empty due to the holiday, so the receptionist was very alert when he entered.

"Hello. May I help you," she asked, sending him a fetching smile.

"I'd like to speak with Dr. Lucy Galbreth," he said in his deep drawl.

"Through those doors." She motioned to her left with a grin. "Then down the hall to a door marked 'Lounge.' You can just go on in. We're slow today. I think she's reading or something."

There was a woman in the lounge reading, but she couldn't be the one he wanted to see. She looked about eighteen years old. Extremely petite, her blond hair neatly cut close to her face, she had huge doe brown eyes that screamed her innocence. If she were a friend of Meghan's, they'd look like Mutt and Jeff walking down the street together.

"Dr. Lucy Galbreth?" he ventured anyway.

"Yes," she answered, smiling sweetly.

"You're Dr. Lucy Galbreth?" he asked incredulously. He'd been expecting a larger person, maybe dressed in black.

"Yes," she repeated, her smile growing. She was used to people being surprised by her looks. She guessed they pictured someone else when they heard her name.

Long ago she had decided it was the title of "doctor" that always threw them off.

Watching her closely, he merely said, "I'm Michael Ramsey."

The reaction he got was extremely satisfying. The friendly smile disappeared and her eyes and mouth formed huge round circles. She had definitely heard of him from Meghan. What's more, she looked instantly guilty.

"Oh, Lord," she uttered automatically. Lucy hadn't talked to Meghan since Christmas Eve and was still laboring under the impression that Michael knew nothing of Meghan's circumstances. The alarm she felt at seeing him was shocking.

"You're a little smaller than I expected," he confessed, watching her as he advanced into the room.

"You're . . . much, much bigger," she muttered apprehensively. "How did you find me?"

"Henry Alderman took pity on me. I'm hoping you'll do the same. And I think I ought to warn you, I'm in no mood to chase you around this particular bush. I want to know where Meghan is," he said in a quiet, but determined, voice.

"Oh, Lord," she repeated, as she stood and began to fidget with the buttons of her white smock. *How could you do this to me, Meghan? I'm damned if I do and dead if I don't. What can I tell him? He looks so miserable,* she agonized mentally.

She considered him for several minutes, then made her decision.

"Mr. Ramsey," she said, coming to her full five-foot height. "I love Meghan. I've been through a lot with her. I've kept all her secrets. I've supported her every effort. There have been times when I stood by Meghan even when every hair on the back of my neck was standing straight on end and every bone in my body screamed for me to run away.

"She's not . . . there's nothing . . . average or normal

about her. Her looks are outstanding, she's a brilliant attorney, she . . . does everything differently from the way everyone else does it. But probably what I like best about her is that she lives. She does everything she wants to. Don't get me wrong," she cautioned him. "She's not a spoiled child. She never would intentionally set out to hurt someone, but she gets these ideas and come hell or high water, if she can pull it off without interfering with the rest of the world, she does it. Do you want an example?" she asked, hoping to try to help him understand Meghan better.

He shrugged. "Okay. If you'll eventually get to what I want to hear."

"Two years ago Meghan suddenly became possessed with a need to learn how to snow ski. That's not so unusual in itself, however it was June. No snow. But she had to learn, right then—not six months later. She was going to fly to Austria, but getting a passport took too long. So she took two weeks off and flew to Mt. Hood in Oregon to take skiing lessons in July," she finished.

Michael just grinned and gave an indulgent shake of his head. "So, she's impetuous. What's your point, Dr. Galbreth?"

"Lucy," she instructed him. "My point is that she's not only very bright, she can also be extremely stupid sometimes. She's impulsive, mule-headed, terribly impertinent, and completely lovable if you accept her as she is."

She gave him a measuring look and reluctantly continued, "I've never betrayed Meghan before, and I wouldn't now, except that she's gone too far this time. She's making a terrible mistake. You love her, don't you?" she asked, point-blank.

"Yes," he answered in the same manner. Then he asked, "Where is she?"

"She's in New Bedford—at her aunt's house. I'll give you the phone number." She sighed, hoping for the

sake of her friendship with Meghan that she was trusting the right man.

"I'd rather have an address. She can be a little slip-
pery on the telephone," he said, giving Lucy a friendly
grin.

She wrote down the address and handed it to him
without speaking. Her anxiety over her decision to trust
him was evident in her fidgeting fingers and warm
brown eyes.

"Thank you, Lucy. I do know what this may have
cost you. I'll try to avoid any mention of our talk today," he promised.

Lucy laughed wryly. "If you show up on her doorstep,
you won't have to mention it. But you could do me a
favor."

"What's that?" he asked. At this point he'd do almost
anything to repay her trust.

"When you see her, remember how desperate you
were twenty minutes ago to find her. Try to be as kind
and loving and understanding as possible. She's . . .
pretty low on self-esteem these days and you are one of
the reasons why. She thought she was doing the right
thing. She never meant to hurt you."

Michael grinned ecstatically. "Don't worry, Lucy. Everything will work out fine. I guarantee it."

Dawn promised one of those beautiful winter days
when the sun shone and the air was crisp and cold.
Meghan had slept well and woke up feeling revived and
full of energy. She felt a renewal of her old spirit and
lust for life.

Being five-and-a-half months pregnant was great. All
the clothes she had slipped into maternity shops to
buy fit beautifully. Her little bundle had grown rapidly
over the past few weeks, and there was no doubt now
that she was very pregnant. The growth of her baby
and the feel of it moving about at night thrilled Meghan.

The morning sickness rarely visited her anymore, and the constant fatigue had dissipated to occasional attacks of drowsiness in the early afternoon. The rest of the time she felt full of life—hers and her baby's.

She hadn't talked to Lucy since Christmas Eve, but Meghan hoped Michael had accepted her rejection and stopped calling. She hoped with each passing day she would forget the emotions he stirred in her, and that the memory of his face, his voice, and the touch of his hands would become less vivid, less tangible. She missed him terribly.

What she had done was stupid and selfish, and she would have to pay for that deed for the rest of her life. The rest of her life without Michael. But the life inside her wouldn't let her regret the act. She loved her baby as she loved and cherished Michael's memory. In times of depression, she took solace in the fact that if she couldn't be with Michael, at least part of him would be with her and in the end, she'd done the right thing in telling him about it.

Dressed in an oversized jogging suit and lightweight thermal underwear, she set out for a brisk two-mile walk into town. She missed her running, but the walks were nice, and if she got tired, she could take a cab home.

In town she refilled the prescription for prenatal vitamins that Lucy had given her and leisurely did some window shopping before heading home.

She saw the silver Mercedes parked in front of her Aunt Kate's house from two blocks away. Oh, Lucy, she thought with a chuckle. Lucy might profess to live the simple life, comfortable but not extravagant, but she always traveled first-class. Meghan used to laugh and tease her about her insistence on taking the more expensive accommodations on planes and in hotels when they traveled together. Lucy had just shrugged, saying, "They're more comfortable." Renting a Mercedes was just like her.

She increased her pace and acknowledged how lonely she'd been all week. The solitude had been nice at first, but Meghan found that once she was rested and feeling stronger, she needed more diversions to keep her mind off Michael.

She slowed to a near halt when her eyes caught a movement on the front porch, and she became aware of the huge bulk of man sprawled lazily on the steps.

"Aunt Kate says you can get hemorrhoids from sitting on cold cement," she informed him as her legs automatically carried her up the walk. She felt as if she were running on autopilot. Funny the way her body took over when her mind was in a tailspin, she thought absently.

"Now you tell me," Michael said, watching her face intently.

"What are you doing here?" she questioned tonelessly, as she ambled past him toward the door.

"I came looking for you . . . again," he informed her simply. Michael's pentup anger and frustration from the last few days had dissolved rapidly when he had seen her strolling down the street, safe and sound, and as beautiful as ever. She had definitely been surprised to see him, but after all he'd been through, a little enthusiasm would have been welcome, although he'd known better than to expect any. Her expression of doomed resignation, however, had the power to reignite his irritation at the situation.

"Is there any special reason you've come looking for me?" she was asking, her head lowered as she inserted the key in the lock and opened the door. She went into the house, leaving the door open behind her.

"Has this pregnancy gone to your head, or are you just pretending to be stupid?" he demanded, as he followed her into the house.

She threw her package on the coffee table and flopped down into an armchair.

"You know," she said observantly, "you are an incredible man. Not only do you sic a bloodhound on my tail in New York, but you follow me here after I went to a lot of trouble to keep my whereabouts from you. What does it take to give you the brush-off?" she asked curtly. "I'll kill Lucy for telling you."

"Lucy didn't have any choice. I'm twice her height and outweigh her five or six times over. Besides, she loves you. She wants what's best for you too," he said. Ignoring her very unladylike snort of distaste, he went on, "As to my inability to get a message, it would depend on the reason the woman had for brushing me off. If I am repulsive to her, which I don't think is the case here, I'd pick up on it right away and leave. However, if she's trying to get rid of me so she can wallow in self-pity over some little problem she's got, that's something else. I'm a firm believer in the adage that two heads are better than one when it comes to problem solving," he told her in a firm but gentle tone.

"You don't know what you're talking about, Michael," she told him tersely. "The only thing you can do for my little problem now, is make it worse."

He just grinned at her, his eyes twinkling in amusement.

"Go get out of that getup and into something comfortable, and we'll have a nice, long talk."

Meghan stared at him for several seconds. Why was she continually besieged by optimistic people? Was she the only one who could recognize hopelessness when it came up and slapped her in the face?

Although the outfit she had on was perfectly comfortable, albeit a little too warm, she could see she was going to have to deal with this situation once and for all. And Michael wasn't going to make it easy for her.

She sighed loudly and heaved herself out of the chair. "You want some tea?" she asked offhandedly.

"I'd rather have coffee, if it's no trouble," he said politely.

"It's no trouble," she said with an indifferent wave of

her hand. "Because you'll have to make it yourself. I don't cook coffee yet."

"You don't cook?" he asked, his surprise obvious. "Is that why you have the housekeeper?"

Meghan had disappeared down a hallway. Her muffled voice could barely be heard. "No, I don't cook. Not yet, anyway. And I have a housekeeper to keep house. Lucy says I remind her of Pigpen, the comic strip character? She says that there's a little cloud of dirt and debris that follows me everywhere I go." There was a pause, followed by some muted noises from the bedroom.

Michael had made his way to the kitchen and had found the percolator when he heard her say, "I don't usually buy anything white because it gets dirty before I get it home. I've always been sort of amazed at how messy I am. I don't feel like a slob."

Mentally, Michael scratched "domestic" off his list. He finally found the coffee and began making the much needed brew.

"Would you still like some tea?" he called.

"No."

"Where's your aunt?" he inquired loudly.

"She's in Bristol, taking care of a sick friend," Meghan answered with humor in her voice.

A good sign, Michael thought hopefully. She was warming up.

"How long will she be gone?" He tried keeping the conversation light.

"I'm not sure; a month, maybe two."

Meghan was sitting on the edge of her bed, procrastinating. Having Michael there in the house was like a wonderful nightmare. She savored the sound of his voice and the thrill of having him so close by. The longer she put off her appearance in the kitchen, the longer he'd be there. . . . Or so she thought.

"Hey! You need some help back there?" Michael bellowed, his voice full of meaning.

"This is it, Meghan," she whispered, bolstering herself. "Deep breath. Head high. Stay cool, and for Pete's sake, don't cry." Dressed in maternity jeans and a green, blue, and gold knit shirt, she rounded the corner into the kitchen, saying, "That smells great! I'll have to learn to make coffee after I master poached eggs."

"It's easy. Just add coffee and water . . . and . . . plug it . . . in," he faltered, as he turned to find Meghan in the doorway, looking gorgeous . . . and very pregnant. His eyes rounded in shock as he fixed his gaze on her belly.

"Holy cow!" he yelped, his voice several octaves higher than normal. "You're really pregnant!"

"Yes, I know," she said in a calm, quiet voice, as she walked past him to pour herself a cup of coffee.

"But . . . how? . . . when?" he stammered, stunned. "We just . . . it hasn't *been* . . ."

"In the usual way, Michael, almost six months ago," she informed him serenely, adding milk to her coffee.

"The first time," he uttered dumbfoundedly, as the picture cleared. "Then you were . . . when . . . and I . . ." He was completely overwhelmed. He'd made love to a pregnant woman a little over a month ago and hadn't had a clue as to her condition.

"Try and relax, Michael. As your attorney, I can tell you it's not against the law," she informed him blandly. She commanded her legs to walk past him and into the living room and was deeply gratified when they didn't buckle.

"Why the hell didn't you tell me?" he roared in anger and confusion. "I could have hurt you."

Meghan knew a moment of real fear at the tone of his voice, but his eyes held not only fury, but his own real pain at her deception. Yet, somehow she knew he wouldn't hurt her physically. He was simply reacting to his emotions, just as she was trying to hide hers.

Maybe an offensive defense would cool him down and turn him off. Maybe then he'd go away and leave her alone. Maybe it would be best for him to go away with a bad memory of her. Maybe . . .

"Because I didn't think it was any of your business," she stated. "At first, anyway. Later on I figured you'd act this way. Dreaming of marriage and picket fences. The only reason I told you at all was because Lucy felt sorry for you, and I decided to tell you myself before she had a chance to. I've already said you can see the baby after it's born. As for the rest of my life, it isn't any of your business."

"Not my business?" he exclaimed loudly, his jaw set rigidly in rage and frustration. "You think I hired detectives before, and ran you down here myself for fun? It just so happens I'm in love with you! Does that make it my business?"

"No," she uttered, as her heart shattered into thousands of pieces, each with its own painfully raw edge.

He came to her and grabbed her arms in a tight grip. His face was a collage of mixed emotions. He examined her soul through her eyes but didn't seem to be able to get any clear answers. The conflict within him increased until all he could do was give her one head-jerking shake.

"I have to go," he said, still holding her arms. She bit her lip to keep from crying out. "I need to think, but I'll be back."

He leaned over and planted a quick kiss on her forehead before turning to the door. On his way out, he turned back to Meghan.

"You're wrong, Meghan Shay. You involved yourself in my life six months ago when you walked up to my table," he said softly, as the steely edge in his voice cut deep into Meghan's heart with each word. "I'm not going to let you back out of it just because we've had a little accident. The plain fact is, darlin', that you're as much mine as the baby is, and I'll prove it to you."

And then he was gone.

Michael lay awake on his hotel bed, churning it all

over and over in his head. Obstinate red-headed witch. How was he going to make her see reason? How many times had he wanted to hit her in the head with a club and drag her off to his cave? He should have done it. If he had, things would be a lot simpler now.

All her talk about not wanting him in her life was a smoke screen to save her pride, at least that's what he was desperately hoping. Lucy knew Meghan cared for him, otherwise she wouldn't have helped him. Even Henry suspected something was happening, and he hadn't gotten all his hints from Michael.

No, she wasn't as apathetic toward him as she wanted to think. She had cared enough to tell him about the baby. If he could get her to admit she cared about him, they could move on from there.

How had Lucy described her? "Impulsive, mule-headed, and terribly impertinent." It would take someone even more so to get her to see reason, and Michael knew Mary Meghan Shay had met her match.

Ten

Meghan had mentally chastised herself between bouts of tears throughout the night. An exhausted sleep had finally taken her, but not until she had seen the first light of dawn. She slept deeply and had to fight her way back to the land of the living to put an end to an annoying noise.

"Buzz."

There it was again. The alarm clock hit the floor and bounced several times, landing on its side in silence.

"Buzz!"

Meghan stuck her head under the pillow, only to discover muffled buzzes were more aggravating than clear ones.

"Damn," she mumbled.

"Buzz."

"I'm coming," she said, groaning as she dragged herself out of bed. With eyes bleary from sleep and swollen from crying, she had to feel her way to the source of her irritation. She stubbed her toe on the coffee table and let loose a string of expletives that always seemed to make her father and brothers feel better in times of stress.

Finally, wearing nothing but a pair of oversized men's

pajamas and a scowl, she flung open the front door to find a grinning Michael waiting on the stoop.

"Good morning. Love the pajamas," he greeted her cheerfully. He picked up a suitcase and started into the house.

"Hold it," she said, the fog in her mind lifting enough to realize that Michael wasn't supposed to be there. "Why are you back?"

"That's obvious. I'm moving in here," he told her matter-of-factly.

She glared at his suitcase, then back to him. Running one hand through her hair to get it out of her face, she said, "I can see that you think you are, but I want to know why. I neither need, nor want you here."

"Tough," he said, pushing past her into the living room.

"Now look here," she started angrily. She closed the door to keep the cold air out and turned to face her intruder.

"No, you look here," he said in an equally angry tone, his size and strength lending it more weight. "You can't cook. You can't take care of this house. And you're in no condition to be alone. What if something happened and you couldn't get to a phone for help? You owe it to the baby at least to eat right and be careful. I'm here to see you do both."

"I don't need your pity, and I can manage very well without you. I did for years before you ever came along," she shouted.

"Look where that got you," he noted softly but pointedly.

"Low blow," she called. She couldn't throw him out physically and she wouldn't go as far as calling the police. And although she shouldn't, she wanted him to stay.

"My aunt will be back soon. I'll be fine until then," she said more reasonably.

"Okay, we'll decide what we'll do next when the time comes, but for now I'm staying."

"You really don't need to," she continued to argue halfheartedly.

"I'm staying." His position was firm.

"Suit yourself," she said with feigned indifference. Then as an afterthought, she added, "On one condition."

"What's that?" he asked, curious.

"You have to teach me how to make everything you cook while you're here," she bargained.

Grinning broadly, the thrill of victory in his eyes, he nodded. "It's a deal."

"Don't sound so cheerful," she warned. "It took Lucy's mother two years to teach me how to make a peanut butter and jelly sandwich."

It didn't take long for Michael to take over and make himself comfortable, and Meghan didn't offer much resistance. All her life she had been left alone to do for herself. Oh, she knew her father and Connie loved her, but the Shays led an unorthodox life. Her father had always called her to get up for school in the morning, and he would scramble an egg for her while he made his own, and Connie had always made her a sandwich for lunch because he said it would make him late for school to clean up the mess she'd make. But the rest of the time she'd had to manage on her own. She had been responsible for making sure her clothes were clean. She had watched the clock so she wouldn't miss her bus, because she knew she'd have a long walk ahead of her if she did. The only time her family had questioned her about school was when she brought home a poor mark on her report card. The only time they had asked what she did with her free time was when she'd been in trouble. During the periods she'd maintained high grades, she was able to involve herself in some well-planned mischief as she floated along through life, taking care of herself.

It had been the same in high school and college.

Maybe more so, because by then she was skipping breakfast, buying her lunch, and had her own alarm clock.

Oddly, she had never resented her life. She'd grown up to be a strong and independent woman. She hadn't felt neglected because Connie and Donald had been raised the same way. It was just the way things were at her house. She always knew, deep inside her, that if she'd ever truly needed them, her father and brothers were there for her, and they loved her very much in their own way.

Meghan had to admit, though, having Michael around to take care of her was pure luxury. She was certain the feeling was pregnancy-related, but it was wonderful nonetheless.

He showed his concern and caring in little ways that Meghan found quite endearing. "Have you taken your vitamin? . . . How many cups of coffee have you had today? . . . Here's your third glass of milk. . . . Time for your walk. . . . Put on a hat."

Meekly, she put up with it all, loving his attention, happy to be able to listen to his voice and see him whenever she wanted to, thrilling to the very core of her being whenever he happened to touch her, and thankful that he did so often.

An easy camaraderie developed between them. It was a time spent learning about and getting to know each other. A time in which their love grew stronger through friendship, understanding, and acceptance. A time during which their passion for one another grew stronger, but both of them suppressed it for fear of upsetting the new-found balance in their relationship.

Michael discovered Meghan was indeed only human. Although not the complete slob she had painted herself to be, she was untidy. She made her bed and washed dishes, she even vacuumed and dusted, but she scattered things from one end of the house to the other. Her shoes and clothes were dropped and left at will, as were books and magazines; teacups, and lunch plates never seemed to wind up in the sink. At first she'd made a valiant effort to pick up after herself, but as she relaxed and became more comfortable with him, the debris began to gather.

She was completely inept in the kitchen. She tried, but it didn't come easily for her. First he taught her to brew coffee. She did that well when she remembered to plug in the percolator. After three tries at teaching her to poach eggs, he'd gone out and bought her an electric egg poacher, so all she had to do was wait for the little red light to go out. Her aunt had used her oven to make toast, which was too much for Meghan, who needed to keep her eyes glued to the egg poacher. So he bought a toaster.

"Look at this," she called triumphantly one morning as she entered the room. She was carrying his breakfast on a tray. "Coffee hot, O.J. from a can, a beautifully poached egg, and toast. My first meal."

Through sleep-blurred eyes, he noted the toast was cold, because the butter hadn't melted, and the egg was slightly overdone on the inside, but he grinned and ate everything with relish.

The days slid by and the time for her seventh-month checkup arrived. She wanted to go alone, but he insisted on taking her, saying he had to do a couple of errands downtown anyway. In the end he got his way. In answer to his questions, she had explained that the actual time she would spend with the doctor was short. All he did was listen to the baby, measure her abdomen, and ask her how she was feeling. But when she was called into an examining room, Michael simply got up and followed her.

"Michael," she whispered angrily, when the nurse had left them alone, "you've got a lot of nerve. You . . ."

"Shh," he broke in. "Indulge me. I've been feeding you and that baby for weeks. I just want to hear it."

Dr. Madisen was a kindly old gentleman who encouraged the husband to take part in his wife's pregnancy and the birth of their child, much to Meghan's chagrin and Michael's delight. He apparently had a very short memory, because she had told him a month ago she wasn't married.

He made a special trip to get a dopscope so Michael could hear the fetal heart. The faint, rapid beat filled the room as Meghan lay on her back with her huge belly exposed.

At first she was mortified for Michael to see her uncovered, but he only winked at her, amused by her embarrassment.

"Come here and feel this, Mr. Shay," the eager doctor instructed. Without hesitation, Michael joined him on the opposite side of the examination table.

"If you put your thumb and fingers here, you'll be able to feel your baby's head," the doctor said, demonstrating the technique low on Meghan's pelvis for the would-be father.

Eagerly but gently, Michael pressed his fingers exactly as the doctor had as he glanced at Meghan's face. There was no amusement in his expression now, only wonder and reverence at what was growing inside her body.

Minutes later they shared their feelings of overpowering awe as they sat and listened to the steady thumping of their baby's heart once again.

"That's incredible," uttered Michael as a slow grin spread across his face.

"That it is," agreed the doctor. "Even after all these years," he said with an indulgent smile. "As far as I'm concerned, there's still nothing in this world that beats a birthing. Now that's what I'd call a natural high," he said with a laugh. "You'll be going to the Lamaze classes, won't you?" he asked Michael.

"Of course," agreed Michael readily, purposely avoiding Meghan's angry glare.

"Good. Good. My youngest daughter-in-law teaches the class at the hospital. I think you'll both enjoy it."

"I'm sure we will," answered Michael.

"Mr. Shay, nice meeting you. I'm always glad to see a father get involved in the birth of his child. There's a special bond that develops in the first few seconds of life, and I've always thought the fathers ought to get in on it. Call if you have a problem, Meghan," he said, and then he left.

"No!" Meghan said emphatically when the door closed. "I told you before, Lucy's going to be my partner."

"That's fine," he agreed. "But I'll go to the classes with you so we can practice at home. The books I've read all say you have to practice, otherwise your concentration will be broken too easily. You want to do this right, don't you?"

"Yes, but . . ."

"Well, how will I be able to help if I don't know what to do?" he asked, breaking into her objection. "You want to be prepared when Lucy gets here and it's time to deliver our baby, don't you?" he questioned, letting her think whatever she wanted to, knowing that he *would* be her partner . . . in all things, including the birth of their baby.

She sighed her defeat loudly, while Michael smirked his victory.

That evening Aunt Kate called.

"Who is the young man that answered the phone, dear? His voice is divine. Where's he from? Texas?" was her aunt's salutation when Meghan came on the line.

"Yes, he is. His name is Michael Ramsey. He's visiting," she spoke loud enough for Michael to hear. "When are you coming home? How is Freddy doing?"

"Not well at all, dear," her aunt said sympathetically. "Last week he caught pneumonia. He's much better now, but it left him as weak as a kitten. I would hate to leave him like this, and of course, he'll need help when he goes home. Are you all right, dear? Will your friend be in town a little longer? I don't like thinking about you being alone. Your time is drawing near."

"I'm fine, Aunt Kate," Meghan assured her. "Please don't worry about me."

Michael passed by her on his way to the kitchen for more coffee and winked at her. He signaled that he was pleased her aunt wouldn't be back too soon.

"Then your friend is staying a while?" her aunt pursued.

"Well, I don't know," she put her off vaguely.

"I'm sure he would if he knew the circumstances. He has such a nice, kind voice. Is he tall?"

"Yes, Aunt Kate, he is tall." She heard a rumbling chuckle from the kitchen.

"Do you think he'll stay with you until I get back?" Aunt Kate was nothing, if not persistent.

"I don't know, Aunt Kate. I suppose so." Meghan rolled her eyes skyward fatalistically.

"Would it be easier for you if I asked him to stay. I know how proudly independent you are, but you really should have someone with you, dear."

Meghan turned to the wall and lowered her voice. "No. No. You don't need to ask him. I'll . . ."

"Ask me what?" whispered Michael in her other ear.

Startled, she swung around to look into his face. Their gazes held, hers cautious, his jovial, as he reached out and gently took the phone from her.

Michael exchanged pleasantries with Aunt Kate while watching Meghan. During the ensuing conversation the laughter in his eyes was joined by something more—a deep affection and possessiveness that sent tingles racing up and down Meghan's spine. She had seen it often in the past few weeks and was leery of it. She knew she shouldn't let him think their relationship was permanent, but she couldn't seem to help herself as her eyes mirrored his emotions.

"Yes, she certainly is," he was saying. "I agree completely. . . . No, no problem at all. I've a lot of spare time right now, and there's nothing else I'd rather be doing. . . . I'm a publisher. . . . Oh, yes. I make plenty of money. . . . I know she is. . . ." He nodded and winked at Meghan. "If that's all right with you, Kate. . . . Oh, completely honorable. . . . Yes, I do. . . . I will. I promise. And you just relax and take good care of Freddy. Meghan's in good hands. I'll take good care of her."

Michael hung up the phone, never once taking his gaze off Meghan's face. He reached out one big hand and laid it on Meghan's cheek. He tenderly caressed her skin with his thumb, savoring its warmth and softness. Meghan's heart beat accelerated and she opened her mouth slightly to draw in extra air. She felt bound in gentle tethers as she stood looking up into his face. Against her better judgment, she wanted him to kiss her. She wanted him to take her in his strong arms and never let her go. She needed him to love her. She craved his touch and longed to touch him in return.

Michael stood looking down at Meghan, reading her like a book. He realized he wanted more than her body, he wanted her trust, her love. He would possess her soul as she did his.

"Your Aunt Kate is my kind of lady," he said in a tight voice, breaking the spell. "She told me to feel free to move in here with you. As long as I'll be watching out for you, it would be more convenient that way."

"Ha," she snorted, turning away in disappointment. "Sometimes I get the feeling the whole world is conspiring against me."

"Maybe you should learn to trust the people who care for you. Our motives wouldn't seem so suspicious then," he said, following her into the living room.

She turned on him in surprise. "What makes you think I don't trust you?" she blurted.

"You want a list?" he challenged.

She considered him for several seconds, then she

warned him, "Has it ever occurred to you, Michael, that maybe *I'm* the one *you* can't trust, but that I might care enough about you to want to save you from a great deal of pain?"

She didn't wait for an answer. Her heart was filled with despair, and she could feel the tears welling in her eyes. She turned and beat a hasty retreat to her room, slamming the door behind her, a clear message that she didn't want to see him.

True to form, Michael ignored her message. This was the closest she'd ever come to expressing her feelings verbally, and he wasn't about to let the opportunity slip by. If making her angry was what it took, so be it.

The door crashed open, and Michael stomped into her room. Meghan lay on her back on the bed, one arm flung over her eyes to keep from looking at him.

"What the hell was that supposed to mean?" he demanded.

"Go away, Michael," she pleaded.

"No," he said vehemently. He came to the edge of the bed and bent down. Taking her by the upper arms, he lifted her off the bed and made her face him. "Tell me," he shouted fiercely, as he gave her a little shake.

"It means I love you, you stupid buffoon," she shouted back at him. "It means you're the most wonderful thing that's ever happened to me and I've ruined it. It means that if you knew more about me, you'd be hurt and hate me forever. And I couldn't bear that," she cried as she burst into tears.

"Ah, Meghan," he whispered, taking her into his arms. "You'll never have to. Nothing you could ever do would make me hate you. You can make me angry at the drop of a hat, that's for certain, but you can't make me hate you. I love you too much."

"You weren't listening to me," she sobbed her protest into his chest.

"Yes, I was. You love me. And I love you," he said simply. "Nothing else you said matters."

"But it does." She looked into his exultant blue eyes. "I've done something that's going to hurt you terribly. Why can't you understand that if I let you stay with me, if we go on together, you'll end up hating me?"

"We've covered that, darlin'! I love you. I'm not going to leave you. What we have comes once in a lifetime. Whatever terrible thing you've done, we can work out together," he explained, his mind made up. "Shh. Let's not worry about anything right now. Let's just enjoy each other. Let's just enjoy being in love."

Meghan stared at him, then shook her head. "You're going to be sorry, but I'm too tired to argue anymore," she said wearily.

"Good. Now get undressed and we'll go to bed."

"What?" she squealed.

Michael grinned. "I'm going to hold you all night while you sleep. I've been cooped up in this house for weeks afraid to touch you for fear that you'd run off to Timbuktu. Now that I know I can, by God, I'm going to."

"No," Meghan stated firmly. She knew the risk of sleeping with him even if he didn't. If he found out that she'd selected him purposely to impregnate her, like he'd pick a bull for his cows or a stud for his mares, he'd murder her. To let him love her and go on as if everything were normal would only compound his hurt in the end.

"Oh, yes," he clarified, his speech thick with passion, as he slipped his arms around her ever-expanding waistline and pulled her close. "Tonight, all night. And tomorrow night and the night after that. Meghan, I love you. Not touching you, holding you, or being able to show my love for you has been killing me by inches."

"But, . . ." she muttered, her heart painfully crashing against her ribs, her soul vacillating between ecstasy and despair.

"No buts about it, darlin'," he murmured as he tried to sway her indecision with soft, feathery kisses.

He nibbled at the corner of her mouth and blazed a trail of heat down her neck before he felt her body begin to relax. He placed tender, adoring kisses on her forehead and eyes and both cheeks, before he took her mouth and masterfully extracted a moan of surrender from her.

Meghan halfheartedly attempted to fight him, but was lost with the first kiss. Every cell of her body, every vaporous thought in her mind, every beat of her heart belonged to Michael. She longed for his touch, craved his kisses, needed to have him near her.

Her guilt was shuffled to the recesses of her consciousness as sensation and desire took over. Promises of telling him the whole truth fluttered by briefly before Michael consumed her completely, and she could contain herself no longer.

Meghan's world began to spin as Michael began to undress her with his big, warm hands. Slowly, as if in a dream, he peeled away her clothes, caressing and kissing every newly exposed inch of her as if paying homage to her beauty.

Of their own volition, her own hands removed Michael's sweater and unbuttoned his shirt so that Meghan could take in the power of his broad shoulders, relish the sinew of his bare arms, and thrill to the erratic rhythm of his heart.

Their lovemaking was long, slow, and mutual. When Michael finally took her, he positioned her body astride his and eased himself into her. He watched her intently for any sign of pain or discomfort. What he saw was her flushed skin, her ragged breathing, her passion-glazed eyes. She moaned her pleasure from deep within her chest. Her pupils were dilated and greener than ever as her head lolled forward and she groaned, "Michael, please."

Slowly, he began to thrust upward. When he was sure he caused pleasure, not pain, he relinquished his control and took his own delicious gratification.

Meghan's world began to spin again until its revolutions became a black swirling mist through which she could see nothing, only feel. Bright lights within her reach beckoned her forward, closer and closer until she could experience their intense heat. For one brief moment of ecstasy, she became one with the light and it shone brighter than ever before. Then she fell away and floated peacefully back to life.

Strong, sure hands lowered her gently to the bed and folded her into a muscled embrace.

They lay silently for a long time, savoring their closeness, yet they were worlds apart. Michael was in heaven. Now that he'd broken through her wall and she had admitted to loving him, all he had to do was convince her to share the rest of her life with him. And he was an optimistic kind of guy, thinking the worst was over.

Meghan, on the other hand, had returned to her own private hell once the haze of passion had lifted. She couldn't let him continue to think the baby was just some wonderful accident. After all, it wasn't an out-and-out lie, simply a slight omission of the facts. All right, a gross omission, but did he have to know everything? Yes, he did, and she needed to tell him if they were ever to have a life together. But how would he react? Being used and lied to wasn't exactly the compliment of the year. Could he understand her motives? Could he ever forgive her? She shivered at the thought of his hatred.

"Cold?" Michael asked as he pressed a warm kiss to her temple. He sat up to pull the covers over her naked body.

"A little," she uttered, cuddling into the warmth of the blankets, suddenly exhausted from the mental and physical strain of their loving.

Michael got up and rummaged through her dresser drawers, finally returning with the flannel gown he'd discovered once before.

"Here, darlin', put this on, and we'll keep you cozy all

night," he said, as he helped her to sit up and get into the gown.

"Michael," Meghan started, feeling compelled to speak by his gentleness and caring. "There's more I need to tell you. I . . ."

"Shh," he cautioned her. He could tell by her face that whatever she was about to say wasn't good, and he didn't want to hear it at this particular moment. He was too happy, too hopeful. There was time enough to deal with little problems now that their major obstacle had been overcome. A whole lifetime. "Go to sleep, darlin'. We'll talk in the morning. Tonight I just want to hold you."

And he did. Wrapped in a long flannel nightgown and Michael's arms, Meghan slept like a baby. Michael didn't succumb to his exhaustion for quite a while. Having her in his arms at last, he lay awake and planned a future for Meghan and the baby and himself.

A week later Connie showed up, unannounced, for a visit. Meghan hadn't had a chance, as yet, to tell Michael about her deliberate seduction of him the night they first met. Every time she thought she had the nerve to tell him, he'd say or do something to interrupt her. Meghan was a little anxious at first when Connie showed up, hoping his disapproval of her actions wouldn't tip Michael off to the truth somehow. She wanted to be the one to tell him in her own way.

Connie was his old, loving self again, and he didn't seem at all surprised when he found out Michael had moved in with her. He later explained this to Meghan in the kitchen, while he got Michael and himself another beer and mentioned purposefully that he'd talked to Lucy recently. He even went so far as to tell her he was glad that Michael was the father of her baby.

In fact, she was a little jealous of the way Michael and Connie got along so well. They rooted for opposite

teams in the football game on television that afternoon. In the evening they cheered together for the
same basketball team. In between games they bragged
about their own athletic prowess. They talked hunting
and cars and hockey and rodeos.

Meghan was sure that when she went to her room
for a nap, the first in a week without Michael, they
didn't even know she was gone.

"How's she doing?" Connie leaned over to ask Michael the question in a low voice when he heard her
bedroom door close.

Michael grinned. "I think she's mad because you
didn't ask her that question, but she's fine. The doctor
thinks it's going to be a big baby, but with her build,
she shouldn't have any problems."

Connie looked relieved, then sat back in his chair.
He studied the air between him and the ceiling for
several seconds, and as if speaking his thoughts out
loud, he said, "Can you believe her doing that? I mean,
wanting a baby is one thing, but to methodically interview and choose the perfect father, and then proceed to
seduce a perfect stranger, takes a hell of a lot of nerve.
To say nothing of how crazy a thing it was to do," he
finished, as if he still couldn't believe it was true.

The silence grew ominous. Connie slowly turned to
Michael and was astonished to see the thunderstruck
look on his very pale face. He knew instantly he had
blundered.

"Oh, Lord," he said, and then, agitated beyond words,
Connie repeated his prayer.

The two men stared at one another, one in horror,
the other in disbelief. It was the former who found
enough words in his head for a complete sentence.

"I thought she'd told you everything." He paused.
"You two seemed so tight, I thought she'd told you and
you'd worked it all out," he explained.

"No, she didn't, so maybe you'd better," Michael said
sharply.

"She'll kill me," cried Connie.

"Then you're in a no-win situation, my friend," the dazed Texan promised dangerously.

Connie heaved the sigh of a doomed man and began telling Michael of Meghan's ambition to have a baby. He told of how she had meticulously planned and executed her scheme. Connie went on to Michael about how she'd gone to the Essex House the summer before and systematically picked out men attending a physics symposium to interview. Meghan had disguised herself as a sociologist or psychologist or something, he said, and when she had finally found the man she thought would be perfect to father her child, she brazenly had set out to seduce him. Connie went so far as to detail her care to make sure the man was from out of town so that she'd never see him again. She hadn't even asked his name. Finally, he tacked on the facts that once she was sure it had worked, she arranged to get time off from work and hired a housekeeper in preparation for the main event.

"Tell me," Michael inquired, "has she ever done this before?"

"No, thank heaven. To tell the truth, I don't think she would again, either."

"Why not?"

"She said she couldn't have gone through with it at all if you hadn't been so nice. She said she was just about to give up the whole idea and go home, when you walked into the lounge. You were going to be her last try, and if you turned out to be as big a jerk as the rest of them, it would have been all over. Turned out you were wonderful and kind and gentle, she said. Meghan felt so guilty afterward, she could hardly look at herself in the mirror."

"When did you find all this out?" Michael asked.

"Not until she came to Boston in September. By then it was way too late."

"And I was never to know?" His tone was thoughtful, but not angry.

"You were supposed to leave town none the wiser," Connie said with a shrug.

He certainly had left town "none the wiser," thought Michael as he walked the streets of New Bedford. To say his anger kept him warm would be a gross understatement. He wondered how many men, including himself, had done that very same thing at least a dozen times. He had met and bedded beautiful women before, maybe even dated them once or twice afterward, only to never see them again—or even think of them again. How many of them had been impregnated accidentally or through their design? The thought was extremely disconcerting.

Oddly enough, taking into consideration Meghan's deep desire to have a child, everything she had done made sense. If Michael hadn't fallen in love with her, he would never have known and therefore he wouldn't have cared or been affected in any way.

He could definitely understand her reluctance to tell him. At first it was probably to keep him from interfering. Later she probably wouldn't have known how to, not to mention her fear of his reaction.

Did she really love him now? Or did she just find it convenient to have the father of her child in love with her. Being as objective as possible, he decided she did truly love him. She had tried to avoid him by running away to have her baby alone, just as she had planned. He had chased her. If she'd thought it was necessary for a child to have a father, she'd have found some other way to get pregnant. No, she had intended that the baby be fatherless.

So how long did she plan to keep Michael in the dark? The question intrigued him. And what should he do in the meantime—confront her and wring her neck, or hope to God she'd find the courage to tell him herself . . . and then wring her neck?

That he still had deep feelings for her, he couldn't deny, but his pride and anger demanded retribution. Understanding her motives and knowing she had meant him no harm were of little comfort at this point. She was like an exotic snake to him, mysterious and repulsive at once.

On the other hand, maybe he should just keep walking, all the way back to New York and out of her life . . . maybe . . .

Meghan got up from her nap to find a sheepish Connie waiting to take his leave.

"I'm sorry I got so mad when you first told me about what you'd done," he apologized. "But it was a damned fool thing to do. You could have been killed so easily, and I care too much about you to have you running around doing things like that."

"I know, Connie, and I'm sorry. And please believe me. I have no intention of ever doing anything so rash again," she replied adamantly.

"Well, hang on to Michael and he won't let you. He's a good man," Connie approved, purposely avoiding telling her that he'd let the cat out of the bag.

"I know," she said in sincere agreement.

"He's going to make a great father for your kid," Connie concluded.

"I know."

Eleven

A couple of days later Michael returned from a trip into town and entered a darkened house.

"Shh," hissed Meghan from the recesses of the couch.

By the light of the television he made his way across the room and sat on the cushion she was patting beside her. She crawled into his arms and draped her long legs out across the sofa.

He held her close, loving the feel of her body next to his. Her lavender scent filled the air. He inhaled deeply and rubbed his chin in the soft hair on the top of her head. One had rested below her left breast, the other made long soothing strokes over her large abdomen.

My lady and my baby, he thought wondrously. The times he'd dreamed of this moment, and yet as glorious as it was, it wasn't as perfect as he'd hoped. If only she'd tell him. If only . . . Maybe if his latest idea to outmaneuver her worked, she'd be able to build up enough faith in him to tell him the truth. And if she couldn't? Well, he didn't relish the idea, but he knew as a last resort he could force her to explain . . . and then what? Time and self-counsel had done much to cool his ire, but the hurt and the desperate hope that Meghan would make things right remained.

He sat silently, relishing her nearness while an old black-and-white movie played on the television. As the hero paced impatiently back and forth on top of the Empire State Building, listening to the shrill sounds of ambulance and police sirens from below, Michael realized that the movie was vaguely familiar to him. It was then, too, that he noticed the tears streaming down Meghan's cheeks.

He gave her an affectionate squeeze and lovingly kissed the top of her head. "I think I've seen this before. What's the name of it?" he murmured softly, so as not to interrupt the drama.

She cast him a look of great disdain and blew her nose. "*An Affair to Remember*." She sighed mournfully. "I've seen it a hundred times."

"And do you cry every time?" he whispered in her ear.

"Every time," she stated, snuggling closer to him.

He held her tighter, trying with all his might to transmit to her the enormity of his love. Consciously or subconsciously, she got the message. She looked at him with moist, bright green eyes. Her hand moved up slowly to rest on the late-afternoon stubble of his beard. Even its roughness felt wonderful to her.

"I love you," she whispered, her eyes telling him how much.

He bent his head and sensuously nibbled on her lower lip. "And I love you, Meghan," he murmured against her mouth.

He explored her lips and knew he'd never tire of the study. He passed his tongue between them and she opened to him willingly, her arm sliding around to the back of his neck. As their kiss deepened, she turned to press as tightly against his chest as she could, given her condition.

Their kisses softened sensuously, then deepened passionately until Michael, feeling his arousal, drew back slightly.

"You're missing your movie," he said on a long breath, as he ran his lips softly across hers.

"I know how it ends," she mumbled against his neck, as her tongue made little swirling motions over his sensitive skin.

"You do know what you're doing, don't you?" His voice was thick and husky.

"I know I'm not knitting booties." She planted kisses down the side of his neck.

Michael moaned his desire and gave her a quick squeeze. "Meghan, I want you so badly . . ."

"I love you, Michael. And I'm fairly certain that if you don't let me make love with you pretty soon, there's a good chance I'll go blind," she said solemnly, her eyes twinkling. "Actually, it's taken all my willpower to keep from attacking you since you came through that door."

"And you're wasting all this perfectly good restraint on me?" he asked, amused and amazed, knowing self-control was not one of her strong points.

"I guess I'm finding it hard to believe you could love someone who looks like one of the World Trade Center buildings," she admitted reluctantly.

Michael laughed. Casting her a sly look of disbelief, he said, "Why, Mary Meghan Shay. Are you fishing for a compliment?"

"A little reassurance, maybe," she said coyly. "Let's face it, I'm no longer the slim and lithe young woman I once was," she added, only half joking.

He gave her a considering smile. Aside from the night when they'd first met, this was the first time she had initiated any closeness between them. Michael thought it was a good sign. Perhaps it meant she was finally accepting the idea that he was part of her life now. Maybe it wouldn't take much longer for her to build up her confidence in their love to tell him the truth. Time and encouragement might be all she needed.

"No, you're not. But do you know the World Trade Center buildings have always been my most favorite buildings? In fact, if we got right down to it, I'd have to admit to being a large-building freak. They've always fascinated me," he said, as he began to unbutton the front of her cotton blouse. "Before I got into journalism, I wanted to be an architect and build skyscrapers all over the world. But someone told me you had to be good in math to be an architect. It was my worst subject."

He lowered his head and pressed his lips to the warm sloping valley between her breasts. Reaching around her, his hands savoring the feel of her smooth, warm skin, he released the catch to loosen her bra, while he said, "But I have never wanted to make love to one. Meghan, darlin'," he said with a shake of his head, "your pregnant body is beautiful. As far as I'm concerned, there is nothing in the world more wondrous or magical than what's happening in your body, to your body, and through your body. But more importantly"—his voice lowered to a deep caress as he looked into her pure green eyes—"I love you. Not just your body or just your brain or just your independence or just your humor or just any one thing about you. I love all of you. Totally and completely."

Meghan's chin quivered and tears welled in her eyes. Her heart throbbed painfully in her throat as she croaked out, "Oh, Michael."

Never had she felt so loved, so cherished, or so wanted. She couldn't remember her life ever being so wonderful or so worthwhile. Michael was everything to her. His touch thrilled her. His embrace made her feel protected and secure. His intelligence and humor befriended her own. Michael's warmth and tenderness touched her very soul. He returned her love freely, and all she'd ever done was to cheat and lie to him.

Shame released her tears. One by one they rolled down her cheeks as she rose to place a gentle, heartfelt kiss on Michael's lips.

"Shh," he soothed. He knew her guilt and the burden she carried. He ached to help her overcome her fear. "Let me love you, Meghan. Let me show you how very much you mean to me. All I want in return is your trust."

He kissed her passionately, drawing out her life's breath and filling his own lungs with it. Meghan gave herself up to the moment. Her body was aquiver with the electric sensations Michael generated with his hands, lips, and tongue.

She couldn't recall them moving into the bedroom or how she lost the rest of her clothes, but her Michael-drugged mind did register the fact that he was standing naked before her. His hands on her abdomen, he took one aroused, deep red nipple in his mouth to tease it further with his tongue and nibble at it with his teeth until Meghan thought she might faint.

The dimly lit room darkened around her, and her knees became like rubberbands. Michael had to lower her gently to the bed.

With his hands and mouth, he conveyed his abiding love for her. His words carved themselves into her heart. His body expressed his need to have her with him for all time.

Together they claimed the magical, mystical land only their coming together had the power to create. They reveled in its splendor and revered one another for making its existence possible. Finally, hand in hand, they returned. Spent. Satisfied. Closer for all they had shared.

"One of your better ideas," Michael murmured against her temple a short time later, his breathing still rapid, skin damp from exertion.

"Mmm," was her drowsy response.

Michael's arm slid down from across her chest to her baby-filled belly. With his big hand he made soothing, circular motions.

He liked touching the baby, she thought vaguely. He wanted his baby, and married or not, she knew, Michael would be a good father. She had certainly made the right choice.

"I can hear your gears grinding. What are you thinking?" he asked in a sleepy voice.

"That movie, *An Affair to Remember*? It reminds me a little of us," she confided.

"How so?"

"Well don't you think our whole relationship just screams of fate? Not the night we first met, but you coming to our firm of all places, your being too dense to know a great brush-off when you get one. It all seems so planned."

"Dense?" he repeated with mock indignation, hoping that with her usage of the word "planned," she was about to tell him the rest of her secret.

"Yeah," she said, and giggled. "Like stupid, dim-witted, not too bright . . ."

"I know what it means," he broke in, coming up on one arm. "And you're wrong. I was smart enough to know a good thing when I had it. Your original idea, however, is probably correct. When historians write about our love affair, they'll call it *Meghan and Michael: A Divine Design*," he finished, grinning.

She returned his teasing smile and pronounced, "I like that."

"The title or my touching you?" he asked, as he continued the lazy circular motion.

"Both," she murmured, as she cuddled closer to him. "You do that a lot. Why?"

"I'm trying to communicate with the baby," he said simply, lying down once more, cradling Meghan in his arms. "I want it to like me."

"Why on earth wouldn't it like you?" Meghan asked, startled by his reply.

"It doesn't know who I am yet. Once it's born, we'll get better acquainted. It'll help me to convince you that the three of us were meant to be together. We were meant to be a family. It's all part of the divine design of things."

"Michael," she cautioned, her tone guarded.

He laid a long index finger across her lips and said, "Wait a second. I can do a better job than that. Don't move."

He padded across the room and dug around in the top bureau drawer until he found a small purple velvet-covered box. Returning to the bed, he took Meghan back into his arms before he spoke.

"I got this for you for Christmas. It was going to be a sort of a . . . think-about-marrying-me ring . . . or if you wouldn't have agreed to that, it was a ring you needed to own anyway. The minute I saw it, I knew you ought to have it. Open it."

Meghan took the box hesitantly. She knew what was inside and she knew what it meant, but she didn't know how she would be able to turn him down—and refuse him, she must. Even she couldn't stoop low enough to marry Michael without telling him the whole truth about the baby. And if she told him, he'd hate her, not to mention the complications his anger would cause.

The ring was stunning. A small rectangular emerald surrounded by diamonds, it was exquisite.

"It matches your eyes," he whispered near her ear. "Please marry me, Meghan. I love you more than I'll ever be able to find words to tell you. I want you . . . I need to have you in my life."

Meghan's eyes were a portrait of agony as she turned to look into his face. She could see his deep love for her, but her guilt wouldn't let her accept it.

"Michael, I . . . the baby . . . I . . ." She faltered on the cold, hard lump in her throat.

"I love you and I love the baby," he assured her sincerely. "I'd be a good father, I promise."

"You'd be a wonderful father," she agreed. "It's just that . . . I . . . I can't."

The misery in her expression tore at Michael's heart. *"Just tell me,"* he screamed at her from inside. *"I'll still love you, and you'll feel so much better."* He considered confessing that he already knew her secret, but her trust was important to him. He wanted her to believe their love could endure all things.

"Darlin'," he said, giving her a tight squeeze. "Think about it. If things are too confusing right now, we'll wait till after the baby's born and everything settles down. I was hoping to get married before the birth so I could give the baby my name, but I can always adopt it later."

Meghan's eyes narrowed in suspicion. "Is that why you're doing this? To give my baby a name? To give it your name? Because if . . ."

"Meghan," he broke in calmly, "I want to marry you because I love you. I planned to ask you when I left New York in December long before I knew about the baby. The baby has nothing to do with it except that it's an added bonus," he told her firmly. "And you can turn me down now if you want to, but I won't give up. I've been waiting all my life for you. I won't lose you."

"Michael," she murmured, her voice forlorn. Meghan believed Michael when he said he loved her. She knew in her heart of hearts it wasn't just the baby he wanted.

"Let's table it for the time being, darlin'. Think about it awhile. I'm content for the moment to settle for our just loving one another. I can wait a little longer until you're ready to make a commitment. Let's get some sleep."

Meghan lay in Michael's arms, but sleep eluded her. Michael, too, apparently was having trouble falling asleep as his embrace remained firm and he continued to caress her skin gently. Finally he softly cleared his throat, and Meghan braced herself to hear whatever it was he'd been ruminating about.

"You awake?" he asked, feeling she was but needing to be sure.

"Yes."

"Why did you say the first night we met wasn't part of the divine design? Can you tell me, yet, what it was all about?" he asked point-blank, wanting, needing to get it out in the open.

"Michael," she started after a long, tense moment, "I do want to tell you. And I will tell you. I just can't right now," she said, giving in to her cowardice and pride.

He sighed resignedly. "Okay. I'll wait."

Long after Michael's muscles had relaxed and his breathing had become deep and regular, Meghan was awake, her mind racing around and around in circles. She loved him with all her heart and soul, but she couldn't marry him without being truthful. She couldn't tell him the truth, because he'd despise her and her heart couldn't bear it. Either way she'd eventually lose him. Maybe she should just tell him and get it over with. She drew in his spicy scent and savored his embrace. She'd rather walk on a bed of hot coals than tell him right now.

The next few weeks passed swiftly and quietly.

Michael didn't bring up his proposal again, but he knew she was thinking about it. She wore the ring on her right hand at his request and often he'd catch her studying it, a look of deep concern on her face, as if she was playing "Should I or shouldn't I?" with the diamonds that surrounded the green gem. He longed to settle the decision for her, but it was hers to make.

Their relationship was loving and companionable, each of them enjoying their time together. They took long walks through the quiet town of New Bedford, with its quaint shops and its network of waterways that surrounded the city. The days were often rainy, but when the springtime sun shone, their love seemed to take on its glow and cheerfulness.

With the Dobson brothers still in control of their

company until after their anniversary issue in August, and Michael's other interests in capable hands, his idleness began to become a little tedious at times. Gestation being a rather slow process, and his part in it relatively minor, he found himself looking for new projects to occupy his time.

Always a challenge was Meghan's reluctant, but determined ambition to become domestic. Her peanut butter-is-peanut butter attitude was enough to make a grown man cry. He taught her to read labels, choosing the brands with the least amount of sugar and the fewest preservatives.

He gave her an ongoing lesson in picking fruits and vegetables, and he frequently had to point out the difference between those you ate and those you threw at politicians. Because he ate mostly fresh fish and lean red meat, the discussion on how to choose pork chops had been difficult, and then his explanation of the benefits of a marbled roast as opposed to one with no fat ingrained had only confused her.

"In this case, not unlike your own," he teased with a gentle pat on her abdomen, "the divine fat makes it more tender and tasty." He bussed her nose with a quick kiss. "It's the gravy you have to watch out for. It'll clog your arteries faster than your peanut butter will."

However, Meghan's idea of going shopping had nothing to do with buying groceries, and she was no slouch when it came to the art of real shopping.

The department stores of New Bedford pushed their doors open wide to her. Since shopping for the baby had been risky in New York, and a baby shower out of the question, a whole new world of unlimited purchases opened up for Meghan.

Shopping, as an art form, required patience and endless hours of browsing to find just the right purchases. She led Michael through aisle after aisle of diapers, six-inch T-shirts, sleepers, bottles, blankets. . . . It seemed to him that the list went on forever.

Michael had a tendency to wander around the store when Meghan became engrossed in deep concentration over subjects like picking out crib sheets with ducks or cartoon characters. After a while he would return with something outrageous such as a pair of twelve-inch denim jeans, a football jersey with a blue and white star on it, or a cowboy hat ten inches in diameter from the boys' department across the way. Meghan laughed the day he returned from the little girls' section with basically the same articles of apparel, plus a ruffled yellow dress with a pinafore for Sundays.

It was during the hours spent buying things for the baby that Meghan could almost imagine herself as a married woman preparing for the birth of the child she and her husband had planned to have long before they took their vows. She enjoyed these visions and refused to face the truth until after the baby's clothes were brought home and carefully put away.

Michael enjoyed the same dreams, only to him they were very real. In his mind, and even more in his heart, he was already totally bound and committed to Meghan. Her presence in his life had already become as much a necessity as the food he ate and the air he breathed. A marriage license with their names on it would be a mere formality, once Meghan realized the trustworthiness of his devotion and accepted his love and forgiveness.

Halfway through her eighth month they started the prenatal and Lamaze classes. Meghan's heart swelled with pride and joy as she watched Michael meticulously and gently bathe and diaper the soft rubber demonstration doll. And she almost choked to death on her laughter the night they discussed breast-feeding.

"We've decided to breast-feed our baby," Michael informed the instructor in a natural, presuming manner. "But there seems to be a lot of controversy over how long to nurse. What do you recommend?"

Twice daily Michael would gather up their pillows and ease Meghan gently to the floor to practice the Lamaze breathing techniques.

"Okay. You've moved into transition. The contractions are stronger and more frequent. Deep cleansing breath," he instructed. "Now let the next deep breath out with short pants."

Meghan let him coach her, but her concentration faltered as she became increasingly aware of the slow, steady circular rhythm of his hand on the small of her back. Little tingles ran up and down her spine as they always did when he touched her. The now familiar feeling was exciting and welcome. Her heart pumped harder in anticipation.

"Whoa. Your pants are too deep. You'll hyperventilate. Let's try it again. Deep breath, followed by shallow, rapid panting," he encouraged.

Again she tried, and again her mind wandered off.

"Meghan," an exasperated Michael called. "You're not concentrating. Where are you?"

She giggled. "Oh, not far from here."

Leaning forward to look at her face, he recognized the distinctive twinkle in her eyes and grinned delightedly. Then he shook his head and admonished, "Business before pleasure, you wanton hussy."

"I was only thinking it would be easier to practice my panting if we were in bed," she defended herself, sticking out her lower lip to pout.

"Sure you were," he mumbled skeptically, as he bent to take her lip between his teeth. The nibble turned into a kiss, and the kiss added fuel to their ever present passion that always lay smoldering beneath the surface of their every glance and touch. "Then again, you may have a point," Michael said in a thick voice. "We could at least try it and see."

Their loving was leisurely and pleasurable. Relaxing

in the aftermath of their passion, their satiated bodies pressed tightly together like a pair of identical spoons, they murmured their happiness and exchanged words of love.

Meghan cuddled her back closer to Michael's chest and moaned with contentment. Michael, his hands splayed across her abdomen and under her breasts, pressed an agreeing kiss to her temple.

"Good Lord," Michael said in wonder. "Did you feel that?"

The baby's kicking and jabbing had become more and more frequent over the weeks. Meghan always relished the sense of awe that accompanied the movements of her child. Several times before, she had beckoned for Michael to come feel the baby, but this was the first time he'd actually experienced it, and Meghan could sense his amazement.

"Yes, I did." She laughed indulgently.

"He's so strong," he said.

"He?"

"Slip of the tongue," he replied, a smile on his face. "How's 'She's got an amazon's punch?' "

Meghan chuckled softly.

"The baby will probably be tall when it grows up, don't you think?" he inquired, his tone casual.

"Well, all the Shays are tall, so maybe," Meghan said drowsily.

"There aren't many dwarfs in my line either," Michael reminded her.

Meghan laughed. "You mean you aren't a genetic accident? I thought everything from Texas was bigger and better than from anywhere else," she teased.

"It's a fact, darlin'," he stated into her hair, and then hoping to make another point in favor of marriage, he said, "You know, our baby is only half Shay. I'll grant you it's probably the best half, but even when they breed horses, the sire's name is as important as the mare's."

It was several seconds before Michael's words came back to him. Meghan had tensed in his arms and seemed to be holding her breath. His eyes snapped shut, and he clenched his teeth at his stupid choice of words.

Meghan's breath had indeed caught in her throat. Could he know what he'd just said? Had he guessed that the baby hadn't been part of the divine design but had actually been planned by her, like one would contrive the mating of a good brood mare?

"You mean like Enoch of Ramsey out of Shay," she tentatively offered, hoping that if she appeared unaffected by his words, he wouldn't know he'd guessed the truth.

"Well, he'd have a terrible time on the S.A.T. exams, writing his name in those little squares. I was thinking of something a bit shorter. I'll take you to court if you name him Enoch, but I think you got my drift," he said, wishing they didn't have to pussyfoot around the circumstances of the baby's conception anymore. Sick of waiting for her to tell him her one last secret, he was still determined that it was important enough to wait.

"I promise I won't name *her* Enoch, okay?" she said, indicating she still couldn't discuss what was foremost in her mind.

Michael sighed dejectedly. How could he get her to tell him? What did he have to do to win her over completely?

In the final weeks of her pregnancy, a strained tension developed between Meghan and Michael.

Michael's frustration forced him to remind Meghan that he loved her and wanted to marry her, with little comments like, "What a gorgeous, sunny day . . . Make a great wedding day, don't you think?" or "When we move back to New York, shall we set up house in your apartment or mine? Mine has more room." His not-so-gentle nudges would bring Meghan up short. Irritation and anxiety riddled her voice as she reminded him that he had promised not to push her into a decision.

He racked his brain to create opportunities for her to tell him. He knew in his heart she'd never marry him unless she told him how she came to be pregnant. He also knew she'd rather cut out her tongue first. Whether she made her final decision before or after the baby was born, she was going to refuse him unless he could somehow force her to 'fess up, and time was growing short.

Meghan's strain was twofold. There was, of course, Michael. Always loving and gentle, always understanding and solicitous of her needs, and always there to unintentionally play on her guilt. She fought to keep her shame suppressed as much as possible, but whole days passed when she could think of nothing else.

With her aunt still nursing her friend Freddy in Bristol, Meghan found her need for Michael increasing daily. The baby's imminent arrival was making itself known.

Meghan's ponderous size made her feel clumsy and awkward; even her maternity clothes were becoming too small. She faithfully propped her feet up and took a nap in the afternoon, but by evening her ankles and feet were swollen to twice their size. She found sleeping at night nearly impossible. She'd sleep fitfully for short periods, then toss and turn, trying to find a comfortable position. Inevitably, Michael would wake in the middle of the night to find Meghan in the living room looking for something to pass the time with, or crying in exhausted frustration.

The thrill of being pregnant had definitely worn off, leaving in its place a constant ache in her back and a desire to have it over with.

Michael, darn him, was always wonderful. Even when she'd whine and snap at him, he'd take it in stride. He'd gently massage her back and feet sympathetically, trying to relieve her of some of the discomfort, and he would make valiant attempts to find things to do that would keep her busy and distracted.

He did all this as well as most of the cooking and cleaning. He was more of a mother than a lover nowadays, and Meghan found herself very dependent on him, trusting him implicitly with her welfare. That rankled her also. She took so much from him and could only withhold the truth in return.

Two weeks before her due date, Michael suggested they take a ride along the coastline. "If you get tired, you can lie down in the backseat or we can get out and walk a little. How about it?" he encouraged.

Meghan was feeling testy and tired. It irritated her that he ignored her scathing remarks and would respond only with patience and kindness.

"I've seen it. Why don't you go and get out of my hair for a while?" she answered sourly.

"It would be more fun if you came along. Besides, I think about half your problem is claustrophobia. You haven't left the house in three days."

"Being shut up in this house doesn't bother me half as much as being cooped up with a happy, cheerful person. Just once I'd like to get up in the morning to a person as grouchy as I am," she snapped.

"In that case, why don't we plan to sit under a bridge and eat kids tomorrow?" he returned humorously.

She grimaced at him.

"Come on, you old troll," he cajoled. "Let's go for that drive. If it's too much, we'll come straight back and you can blow smoke out your ears all afternoon."

"All right," she shouted, slamming her hand down on the breakfast table. "I'll go on the stupid drive, if you'll stop trying to be so damned nice. It's driving me crazy."

"Okay, my bad-tempered, but beautiful witch," he bellowed back.

His staged anger elicited a growl from Meghan as she flounced out of the room to get dressed. Michael simply shook his head and thanked heaven that she had only a couple of weeks to go, because he, too, was running low on patience.

The April sunshine beat down on the car and even though it was still chilly outside, the inside of the car grew warm and cozy.

When Meghan failed to break Michael's good spirits, she finally relented, and, although she was far from happy, her remarks were less caustic. Long periods of silence, the warmth of the car, and its soft vibrations lulled her, and eventually her eyes drooped and closed.

Michael reached out a long arm and gathered her to him. With her head on his shoulder as she slept, he drove miles farther than he'd planned, just so she could get some rest.

When at last she finally woke, it was nearly time for lunch. They stopped at a small, isolated restaurant to eat. Her humor somewhat improved, Meghan agreed to a short walk along the beach before starting back.

The day had become increasingly overcast, although it hadn't begun to rain yet. The beach was deserted. It was as if they were alone on earth as they walked hand in hand in the sand.

"I'm sorry I've been such a bear to live with lately," Meghan said, sighing heavily.

"Don't worry about it, darlin'. I can't even imagine how I'd feel if I ached all over, couldn't sleep, and had to deal with a belly five times its normal size. It'll be over soon, and in the meantime I'm a big guy. I can take it."

"That's just the point. You shouldn't have to," she said contritely. "You've been nothing but kind to me and all you get in return is my sharp tongue. You don't deserve it."

"Well, let's say you owe me one. Sometime when things aren't going real well for me and I snap at you, you love me a little extra and be patient with me, and we'll call it even. Okay?" His gray eyes twinkled with his great love for her, and Meghan again blamed herself for all she'd done to him. How could she love him so much and treat him so badly?

"I love you, Michael," she said softly, but loud enough to be heard over the surf.

"And I love you, darlin'." He pressed a kiss to her temple and left his arm around her shoulder as they ambled along a short stretch of beach.

In no hurry to return, they perched themselves on one of the large boulders that cluttered the deserted sands. They talked of kings and fairy wings and other equally insignificant, but fascinating things.

"Will you be all right if I leave you alone tomorrow?" Michael asked casually, as they sat wrapped in each other's arms watching wave after wave roll onto the beach. "I talked to the Dobsons yesterday, and they'd like me to come in for a staff meeting even though I won't actually be taking over for a few more months."

"I'll be fine. I'll even try and work on an attitude adjustment while you're gone. Maybe the time apart will make me appreciate you more when you get back." She smiled up at him. "When will you leave?"

"Early in the morning and I'll be back in the late afternoon. And please, don't go into labor while I'm gone," he pleaded, as he pressed a kiss into the hollow of her neck.

On the ride back they stopped for a light supper, which brought them home late. Meghan was bone weary, but experience told her that the ache in her back would only keep her awake if she went to bed.

"You go ahead," she told Michael, after he offered to massage her back for her. "I'll do the exercises—they usually help, and a soak in the tub will fix me up as good as new. You're exhausted. Go to bed."

"The offer stands. If you change your mind, just yell," he mumbled, sleepily, as he grazed her lips with his and headed for bed.

"If you hear me yelling, it's because I'm stuck in the tub," she said.

The long day and the hot bubble bath did much to repair Meghan's taut nerves, if not the pressure in her lower back. Propped with pillows on the couch, she suddenly realized her thoughts and emotions seemed clearer to her than they had in months. There was no inner debate, only a calm tranquility in which her questions seemed easily answered.

Did she love Michael? Yes. Did she want to marry him and spend the rest of her life with him? Yes. She'd already decided she was ready to have and take on the responsibilities of a baby, but a husband too? Definitely. Was there any way she could get out of telling him the truth? None. She loved him. He deserved to know . . . and there was always that one-in-a-million chance he might understand and forgive her. If he didn't? At least she'd have the comfort of knowing that she loved him enough to tell him the truth.

Half-asleep, Michael felt the bed sag and realized vaguely that Meghan was either coming to bed or getting up again because she couldn't sleep. His subconscious waited to see in which direction she was going, but when there was no further movement, curiosity forced him to come fully awake to check on her.

Meghan sat on the bed watching Michael sleep. Could anyone mean more to her than this gentle giant who looked so like a little boy when he slept? Could she learn to live without him? Was there the slightest chance he'd forgive her?

Slowly his eyes came open and he spoke, "Are you okay, Meghan?" he asked her softly.

"Yes. I'm fine," she returned with equal softness.

"Then come to bed, darlin', and I'll . . ."

Michael was cut off mid-sentence when Meghan laid her hand firmly over his mouth. Meghan couldn't risk his saying something kind or loving and destroying her resolve. She needed to tell him the whole truth and she couldn't let him stop her this time.

"Michael, I don't expect you to forgive me for what I'm about to tell you," she started quietly, calmly, "I can only hope you can find it in your heart not to hate me too much."

Michael mumbled something under her palm and raised his hands in a questioning manner, but made no attempt to remove the seal across his lips.

Meghan simply continued with her cleansing confession. "The night we first met wasn't part of any divine design, Michael, it was of my design. I planned it. I don't know if you'll be able to understand this, but for years now, more than anything, I've wanted a child of my own. A baby I could love and nurture. It was a need so deep I felt compelled—driven to fulfill it.

"When you refused to enter my life under normal circumstances, I was forced to go out and find you. I set out that night intending to get pregnant. I interviewed nearly two dozen men before we met. You made it all so easy with your humor and gentleness. You'll never know how often I've regretted interfering with the original design. If I'd waited a few more months, you'd have come to see me at the office and we could have avoided this mess. Instead, I botched the best thing that's ever happened to me. I used you like a stud horse; I denied you the right of choosing the mother of your baby. I've lied and cheated you out of one of the most important events of your life. Worst of all, what I've done has been degrading to your integrity and character and . . . all I can do is say I am most truly sorry for what I've done," she finished on a note so eloquently sincere that Michael was stunned by the force of it.

Never in his wildest imagination had he thought it possible to love one person as much as he loved Meghan at that moment. So overpowering were his emotions, that he was unable to move or speak. When Meghan's hand slowly fell away from his mouth, all Michael could do was stare at her through the darkness of the night.

After a long, tense silence, Meghan finally stood and said, "I know you're probably so mad it's all you can do to keep from killing me right now, and we're both tired. I'm sure your anger won't have burnt itself out by morning. Maybe it would be better if we discussed this then," she offered as a tentative solution to Michael's silence, and turned to leave.

Michael reached out and firmly grabbed her wrist. "I love you, Meghan," he uttered.

"Did you hear what I told you or did you just wake up?" she asked, frowning. This wasn't exactly the reaction she'd expected.

"I heard," he said, fighting the urge to draw her into his arms and love her so intensely and for so long that she'd never doubt his love again. But he knew what it must have cost her in energy and emotion to have told him the truth, and they were both exhausted. Morning would be soon enough to tell her he'd known for weeks and that his anger was long ago spent. Her confession only strengthened the bond between them. "We'll talk in the morning."

"Okay. Good night," Meghan said bewilderedly, as she backed out of the room. Wouldn't this man ever react the way he was supposed to? Why wasn't he yelling and screaming at her like he should be? Even Job had his limits.

Confused and a little dazed by Michael's lackluster response to the fact that he'd been used like a common stud horse, Meghan settled back into the couch and tried to get comfortable. Unable to decipher Michael, she became aware that her own inner turmoil was at last at an end. She had told him the truth.

With her mind and guilty conscience acclimating to the new condition of being right with the world once again, a warm satisfaction seeped into her pores and made her feel cozy and lighter than she'd felt in months. Oh, she knew Michael might very well raise the roof yet, as he ought to. There were a number of ways Michael could vent his anger once her words had finally sunk in, but the freedom Meghan felt induced a strength that made her believe she could survive any harsh criticisms he would eventually dole out.

She slept well, only vaguely aware of the intermittent discomfort in her lower back.

Twelve

The first time the phone rang, Meghan burrowed herself into the pillows and blankets hoping Michael would answer it before she came completely awake. By the fifth ring it was clear she'd have to get it herself. Where was he, anyway? she wondered.

"Hello," she mumbled drowsily into the receiver.

"You're home," stated a familiar voice. "I was worried when I couldn't reach you yesterday. I thought I'd missed the big event."

"I'll refuse to have this baby without you," Meghan reassured Lucy. "I'll keep my legs crossed till you get here."

"Dreamer. You're not going to have much say in it when the baby decides to be born," she said with a laugh. Then with more consideration she added, "On the other hand, none of your actions since last summer has been exactly normal or run-of-the-mill. And I must admit, I admire your courage. I thought you weren't going to tell Michael."

"Tell Michael what?" Confused, Meghan brushed her hair out of her face and tried to pay close attention to the conversation and less to the pain in her back, which seemed stronger now than it had last night.

Maybe she shouldn't have slept on the couch, she thought, resigned to another long day of discomfort.

"I thought you weren't going to tell Michael how you planned your pregnancy," explained Lucy.

"What?" Warning signals started to go off in Meghan's mind. She felt the blood drain from her face as her heart began to pound and her hands became clammy. How did Lucy know she'd told Michael the whole story?

Lucy, picking up on Meghan's alarm, began her story cautiously. "When I couldn't reach you for so long yesterday, I thought maybe you'd gone into labor. I called the hospital, but you hadn't been admitted, so I tried the pub, hoping Pop knew where you were. Connie answered. He said I shouldn't worry because Michael was with you and he'd take good care of you. Well, one thing led to another, and in the course of the conversation we decided Michael was a good man for you and I mentioned that I wished you could be completely truthful about the baby with him, and . . . well . . . Connie said Michael's known for weeks."

"What?" Meghan repeated, panic evident in her voice.

"That's what Connie said. He said Michael knew all about the baby's conception and that he was taking it very well."

"But how? I didn't tell him. Did Connie tell him?" she asked.

"I don't know. Connie said he knew, and I just assumed you'd gone crazy and told him," Lucy explained.

Meghan vacillated between gross humiliation and wild, furious anger. The two emotions grew until they merged into overpowering rage. Her grasp on the phone turned her knuckles white and her muscles trembled in response to her wrath.

"Meg?" Lucy called into the silence. "Meghan? Are you there? Are you all right?"

"Yes," came her terse reply.

"What are you going to do, Meghan?" an anxious Lucy asked.

"Before or after I kill Michael?"

"Meghan . . ."

"He's been toying with me. Taunting me! Playing on my guilt," she ground out through clenched teeth. "I'm going to kill that man."

"Meghan. Don't do anything stupid. I called to let you know I got some extra time off; Jeff is with my in-laws and I'm on my way. I'll be there by noon. Don't do anything until I get there," Lucy pleaded.

"If you think I'm going to stay here so he can torture me some more, think again. I'm on my way to Boston," she shouted impulsively. She heard the beginning of Lucy's protest about traveling so close to her due date, but she hung up the receiver determinedly. She knew she would never be able to handle logically anything that Lucy had to say, especially if it meant staying in New Bedford. Boston was less than two hours away and she felt fine except for the incessant backache. She still had two whole weeks before the baby was due, and it was practically penciled in stone that first-time mothers had a tendency to be overdue. She'd be fine. Lucy worried too much anyway. All Meghan knew for sure was that she couldn't face Michael—not now, not today. She had to get away, she decided more firmly, as she stomped back into the living room to gather her things.

She found Michael's note propped neatly against the planter on the coffee table.

Morning, my beauty,

Didn't have the heart to wake you. Have I ever told you how beautiful you are when you sleep? Eat something decent for lunch, and I'll bring dinner home with me. I love you.

Michael

P.S. About last night . . . I think we ought to include the first night as part of the design. Otherwise you wouldn't have been at the Essex looking for a man, and I wouldn't have been there to be found. Think about it.

M

"Yeah, right," she said dismissively, wadding up the note and throwing it on the floor. "That's why you didn't flinch a muscle when I told you last night, you heartless fool," she concluded disgustedly.

Then the phone rang a second time.

"Good. I'm glad you're up. I hope you slept well," came Michael's cheerful voice. "I'm just calling to check on you and to see if you want me to stop by your apartment and pick up anything?"

"Michael Ramsey," Meghan ground out, her voice increasing in volume, "you can go straight to hell."

Michael stood frowning at the receiver after the line suddenly had gone dead.

"What the hell was all that?" he wondered aloud.

Either she got up on the wrong side of the couch, or something was grossly amiss in New Bedford, he determined. And having been around the block several times with Meghan, he knew exactly who to turn to to find out what was wrong.

"Damn," he said several minutes later, as his forehead came to rest on the arm he was dangling over the pay phone. "Now what is she going to do, Lucy? And where does she get off making me the heavy in all this? I thought it would be easier on her if she told me herself." With his own anger rising to the surface, he added hotly. "She's damned lucky I didn't light into her the night I found out."

"I know, Michael," Lucy sympathized with her new friend. "I think she's more angry at herself than she is with you. To tell you the truth, this is very unlike her. She might run away to keep from hurting you, but she'd never flee from a good fight." She hesitated briefly, then went on. "Look, I was just leaving for the airport. I'll be in Boston by noon. I'll talk to her . . . try to explain things for you. She's just full of pride, but she'll come around."

Michael had interrupted with a surprised "Boston," but Lucy hadn't stopped to explain. When she finally stopped speaking, a pensive Michael spoke softly. "Thanks anyway, Lucy, but I think it's time Meghan and I had this out between us, once and for all."

Meghan had packed and was laboriously loading up her car before the steam generated by her anger finally evaporated and cleared her vision. It wasn't Michael she was angry with, but herself.

She had no right to take her humiliation out on him. He hadn't been nearly as cruel as he could have been when he met her again at the office. He hadn't blinked an eye when he so unceremoniously discovered he was going to be a father, and had easily forgiven her for not telling him sooner. Michael must have also found it in his heart to pardon her initial deception, or she surely would have heard about it before this. And he'd given her plenty of opportunities to tell him herself.

No, Michael had been nothing if not loving and forgiving. She owed it to him to stay and wait and hear him out, but, to use his expression, she felt lower than a snake's belly.

Shays never ran from a problem; they faced it head on. Well, she was a Shay and she'd withstood Michael's anger when he'd tracked her down before—twice! She had mustered the courage to tell him about his baby and about its conception, but all she wanted to do this time was to find a nice, safe hole to crawl into. She didn't have the strength to face Michael now. She planned to eventually, but just not today.

The safest hole she knew of was in Boston. She left Michael a letter telling him where she was and explaining that she knew they had a lot to talk about and that she'd be back in a few days.

Meghan had reached the outskirts of Boston before she realized how tense and anticipatory she was. What was she waiting for? Michael to show up in the rearview mirror? No, it would take hours before he discovered her whereabouts. If he stayed true to form, though, he'd show up eventually. Then what?

Well, it didn't matter now. She'd be on solid ground with Pop and Connie and Donald to back her up and keep Michael away from her.

Her body gradually tensed once again. Slowly, the pressure in her lower back increased to a very uncomfortable, but not painful degree, then ebbed away.

She was aware that while her mind had been drenched in self-pity, her body had been monitoring the intermittent spasms in her back. She glanced at the digital clock on the dash. Twenty minutes later she felt the familiar tensing in her body and the intensifying pressure along her lower spine. After another twenty minutes the experience repeated itself.

"Oh, Lord," she prayed aloud, as she pulled up outside the private entrance to the pub. "Not now. Not today."

Although her father and brothers were glad to see her, they were obviously concerned with her pallor and the lines of exhaustion in her face and were even more distressed, it seemed, with the absence of Michael, who, by way of Connie, had become a frequent topic of discussion between the three Shay males.

"He shouldn't have let you come all this way alone this close to your time. He shouldn't let you travel at all," her father chastised Michael.

"He's not my keeper, Pop," she offered. "He's not my

husband, or my brother, or my father. He has no say in my life."

While the three Shay men passed cautioning glances at one another, recognizing the first signs of one of her thunderstorms, she announced, "I'm going up to lie down for a while. Send Lucy up when she gets here . . . Please."

With that she turned on her heel and marched to the foot of the steps that led to the living quarters above. She stood evaluating the challenge for several seconds, then straightened her shoulders in determination and proceeded up the stairs, stopping frequently to catch her breath.

When she was out of sight, Connie turned toward the kitchen at the rear of the building. "I'll call Michael. If they've had a fight, he'll need to know where she is so they can clear things up."

He was no sooner out of sight when Michael Ramsey walked through the front door.

Michael stood on Temple Street, not far from Boston Common. Normally a very busy street, it was relatively quiet for that hour of the day. With an apprehensive eye, he surveyed the little Irish pub before him and noted the "open" sign in the window.

It was definitely an Irish tavern. The stained glass windows held a hundred shamrocks displayed in various positions throughout the colorful glass. Inlaid in the artwork on the door was the name "Shay's," the tavern's only advertisement.

Moving inside, Michael wasn't surprised to find it clean, quaint, and well kept. The place was decorated in dark, vibrant colors from the glass in the door to the deep, warm wood tones of the furnishings. Pewter tankards and mugs hung from several beams in the ceiling. The wall behind the main bar was constructed of more stained glass, lit softly to produce a warm glow. It was a very pleasant, charming little pub.

The barroom was practically empty. A few patrons were scattered about at tables. An older gentleman sat at one end of the bar reading the morning paper as he drank his coffee. At the other end were two of the men Michael was looking for. He recognized them instantly from the photo he had seen in Meghan's living room and from their distinctive red hair.

Michael could hear them speaking in low tones to one another as they nursed their own cups of coffee. He took a seat at the middle of the bar and watched as the older of the two men moved toward him.

He greeted Michael with a friendly smile. "What can I get you?"

"Just coffee, please," Michael replied, feeling oddly anxious and awkward at meeting Meghan's father.

"Need a little hair of the dog in it?" Sean Shay asked absently, as he poured his customer a cup of coffee.

"No thanks. I wasn't bitten last night," he answered. "You're Mr. Shay then," inquired Michael politely, already sure of the answer.

"The one and only. Unless, of course, you count my boys." He motioned vaguely in Donald's direction. "And a few hundred others in these parts. Shay is a pretty common name around here."

"But you're the Shay with the daughter named Meghan, correct?" Michael asked with a smile.

Out of the corner of his eye, he was aware that Donald had come to life and was waiting at attention for his father to speak.

The old man's countenance had undergone a rapid change. Gone was the friendly bartender with the easy manner. He was now tense and suspicious.

"I am Meggie's father. What's it to you?" he asked guardedly.

"I'm a friend of hers," he said casually, acutely conscious of the fact that the burly brother had moved closer.

"Just how close a friend are you?" the older man asked, his eyes narrowing as he observed Michael.

Michael straightened his shoulders and looked Sean Shay in the eye. "Very close. I care very much for your daughter, Mr. Shay. As to the details of our relationship, sir, I don't think they're any of your business."

"They are if you're the father of her baby," Sean said, his temper rising.

Michael swallowed hard, knowing this was the most awkward situation he ever had or would experience in his life.

"Yes, sir," he admitted, giving no outward signs of his nervousness, "Meghan is carrying my child."

A dark thundercloud of anger settled over the old man's brow. "In that case, I'll make use of my right, for the first time, not to serve someone," he said harshly, taking a swipe at the countertop with his bar rag. "Any man not willing to do what's right when he gets a girl in trouble is not welcome in my bar."

"Takes two to tango," said Donald from several stools away, making his own thoughts of Meghan's behavior obvious. The fact that he was enjoying the whole situation irritated Michael.

He gave Donald a measuring look, then pointedly turned back to Sean Shay.

"I'm very willing to marry Meghan, Mr. Shay," he said clearly. "I was hoping she'd have me long before I knew about the baby, but your daughter is the proudest, most stubborn, pig-headed woman I've ever met. She's too embarrassed to marry me," he finished angrily.

"Sorry, Mr. Ramsey." Sean Shay paused, relaxing visibly and taking on a knowing, sympathetic look. Michael gave his first name and the older man continued. "I'm sorry if we came on a little strong, Michael. But you know the old saying 'A son is a son till he takes a wife. But a daughter's a daughter all of her life.' You've come to the right place for help. While she's asleep upstairs, we'll put our heads together and force the girl to see reason."

"Sounds good to me, sir," Michael said, grinning, glad to have an ally.

Sean kept Michael's coffee cup full while he went on to praise Meghan in glowing terms. He told of how spunky and indomitable she was as a child and how proud he was of what she'd made of her life. He related how he'd helped as much as he could with her education, but it hadn't come close to being enough. He mentioned how she had worked her way through Harvard, and all she'd been through to earn her position at the law firm.

Meanwhile Meghan had settled herself on the comfortably familiar bed in her old room. She took a deep cleansing breath and let it out slowly to help her relax. Then she waited.

The back spasms she had come to recognize as early labor pains were still regular and holding at twenty minutes apart.

"I'll just lie here and relax. I still have lots of time, and Lucy will be here soon," she calculated drowsily, as her eyelids covered her tired, scratchy eyes.

Then next thing she knew, her eyes flew open with a start. It took several seconds before she recognized her surroundings, and when she looked at the clock beside the bed she saw that at least two hours had passed. Her attention was drawn to the uncomfortable tightness in her abdomen. She breathed deeply and slowly, and gradually the tension dissipated.

She lay very still, eyes wide with anticipation and fear. The minutes ticked by. After twelve minutes a pressure started at the sides of her belly and increased to cover the entire dome of her abdomen with such intensity that her brow furrowed and her teeth clenched before it began to subside.

This was it, then. Full-fledged labor. She waited out the next twelve minutes and the next contraction just to make sure. She was excited and frightened, happy and depressed all at the same time.

She heaved herself out of the bed. She'd have to go to the hospital soon. The family needed to be alerted, and with any luck at all, Lucy would be downstairs waiting to help her.

Slowly, she made her way down the stairs. She could hear Connie and her father talking on the other side of the doors that led into the bar. Another contraction gripped her at the bottom of the stairs. She seized the handrail for support and took a slow, deep breath in through her nose, exhaling just as slowly through pursed lips. Following the lessons she'd learned in Lamaze class, she repeated the exercise until the pain ended.

"Oh Lord, what have I done?" she thought. *"I don't want to go through with this anymore,"* she added in desperation.

"Connie? Pop?" she called, as she swung through the door into the barroom. "I . . ." Her words caught in her throat as she spotted Michael seated between Donald and Connie at the bar, talking to her father who stood in his usual spot behind the counter.

The four men turned their heads when they heard her. All the humiliation of that morning returned and she momentarily forgot the imminent arrival of her baby. Instead, her instincts of self-defense rose to protect her heart and soul and pride from more anguish.

"I don't recall inviting you here, Mr. Ramsey," she said acidly.

"It's a public pub, Miss Shay," he returned dryly, slipping off his stool and advancing toward her. "And we need to have a little talk."

"Stuff it, Michael," she instructed.

"Meghan. Listen . . ." he started.

"I don't want to listen, Michael. I don't want to talk. I just want you to go. We'll talk in a few days," she stipulated, as she walked around him toward a bar stool.

She could feel another contraction beginning and hoped that if she could sit down and turn her back to him, he would be unaware of what was happening.

The bar was nearly empty again after the lunch rush, and the few stragglers left seemed engrossed in their own lives, and were paying little attention to the drama unfolding at the bar.

Concentrating on the steadily increasing pain in her abdomen, she vaguely could hear Michael saying, "You will listen. I'm not leaving till we clear the air."

Although her teeth were clenched in pain, she only sounded angry when she said, "It's already pretty clear to me, Michael," while in her mind, she tried to calculate the time. It hadn't been twelve minutes since the last one, she realized, and this one seemed worse. More frequent, greater intensity, she recalled from her classes. Oh, great!

"Good," Michael continued, unaware of Meghan's discomfort. "Then maybe you can clear it up for me. This stupid disappearing act of yours has got to stop. I'm sick of the deceptions between us, and I'm sick of your distrust of me. Now turn around and fight me like a Shay," he finished, his voice harsh with frustration.

"Trust," she spat back at him. "That's a laugh. You took my love and trust and made a fool of me. You've known for weeks about me and the baby. About what I did," she stormed, as she turned on the stool to face him, the pain ebbing, her eyes bright with physical and emotional pain. She could feel hysteria slowly taking hold at the frayed edges of her mind. She briefly glanced around the bar in panic. Some of the patrons had turned in their seats to watch the pregnant lady fall apart in front of their eyes.

Meghan didn't care. Her frantic mind generated a rush of super strength. She'd slay this Goliath and walk majestically into the sunset to have her baby.

She straightened her shoulders, drew in a deep breath, and continued her attack. "You knew I tricked you into being the father of my baby and you didn't tell me. You . . ."

Her tirade was interrupted by her shocked father. In

stunned confusion, he injected, "Meghan, what are you saying? Now what have you done, girl?" he finished, his anger rising as visions of the possibilities flashed through his mind.

Meghan released an exasperated sigh and half turned in her father's direction, her eyes still on her original target.

"I planned the whole thing. I didn't even know him," she said tersely. "I picked him."

"Picked him?" her father echoed, too confused to be angry anymore.

"That's right," Michael took up the story. "Out of over five hundred men, she picked me to be the father of her child. She planned it, Sean," he explained.

Over Sean's bellowed, "Five hundred men!" Michael went on to say, "It was a perfect plan, too, except that she didn't take into consideration that I might fall in love with her that night. She haunted me for months, and when I found her again, I was ecstatic. I was determined to convince her to share her life with me. When Connie opened the little can of worms about her grand plan, I was overjoyed and honored that she had picked me. But that's not all I felt," he cautioned, now addressing himself to Meghan again. "I was damned mad you'd tricked me like that." He paused, thoughtfully studying the woman he loved. He took in her flawless porcelain skin, the dark shadows under her pure green eyes, now dulled with fatigue and strain, her wild crop of red hair, so soft to the touch. Always, she was beautiful, but more important, she was warm and loving and strong. He had come to admire and respect the courage and determination that had driven her to such lengths. And he envied the baby she had craved to love.

"I took a walk that night," he continued, "to keep from killing you in your sleep. Halfway around the block I could easily envision my life without you. For a while I thrived on my anger. I plotted several routes of revenge. By the time I was back at the house my anger had burned itself out and the life I could see for myself was an empty shell. Where your loving and laughter had filled me so completely just hours before, there was only an echoing emptiness I knew I couldn't live with. Which meant I couldn't hate you. So . . . on my second trip around the block, I tried to forgive and understand you. Knowing you, I was sure you hadn't deliberately set out to harm anyone. I also knew entrapment wasn't in your plan, because you made no demands and went to great pains to make sure that whoever the father was, he wouldn't get involved. You just wanted a baby," he said emphatically, "and I did understand that and I forgave you your deception."

Michael took several steps closer to her, but they didn't touch. Their audience forgotten completely, he continued. "My third orbit around was riddled with questions like, if you loved me, why hadn't you told me? That one was easy, you did love me and were afraid of losing me. That gave me hope. Then there was, how do we get the truth out in the open? Not so easy!" he said, making the familiar gesture of frustration by running his hand through his hair.

"You are right," he conceded. "I should have just told you that I knew the whole story. But I wasn't playing games. I was trying to give you opportunities to tell me yourself. I wanted you to trust in my love enough to know I'd always love you."

"What I did was so stupid and so wrong, but it seemed so right at the time," she said, her sails suddenly windless. "And I did want to tell you . . . many, many times, but I was afraid to take the chance," she murmured softly, humbled by the relief and gratitude filling her heart and soul. This man's heart must fill his body from head to toe, she thought. Never had she met anyone so loving, so understanding. Her entire being swelled with the love of him as she tensed her body to endure yet another contraction.

"I know, darlin'," he returned. "I should have told you I knew the truth and that it didn't matter anymore, as long as we could be together. However," he said, his tone changing drastically, becoming sharp and vehement. "I'm not the wonderfully forgiving guy you're thinking I am right now. And so help me Meghan, if you ever run from me again or lie or withhold information from me again, you're going to have hell to pay. Do you understand me?" he added, as he took a firm grip on her upper arms, preparing to give her a good shake and then hug her until she popped.

He never got to the embrace. As he took hold of her, Meghan let out a bloodcurdling cry of pain and agony. Everyone in the room gasped loudly, as her legs buckled and she fell against Michael, who uttered a shocked, "Good Lord," in lieu of a lengthy prayer.

"Oh, Michael," she wailed, tears streaming down her cheeks. "I love you so much. Please don't let me die now. Don't let our baby die. Not now!"

"No one's going to die, darlin'," he said, his drawl covering the panic he felt. He scooped her huge body into his arms and started for the door. "How long have you been like this?"

"All morning," she replied wearily.

"How far apart are the contractions?" he demanded, more than a little rattled.

"I'm not sure anymore. I think this is the fourth one since I came downstairs," she answered vaguely, holding on tightly to Michael.

"Dammit, Meghan! Why didn't you say so," he shouted. Then as Meghan's head fell weakly onto his shoulder, his voice softened. "It's okay, darlin'. Tell me when the next one starts, then take a deep . . ."

The door closed behind them. Wrapped up in themselves, they understandably didn't pay any heed to the commotion they left behind them in the pub.

The men who had stood to defend Meghan when Michael had grabbed her and she had cried out in pain were now returning to their seats. The room was abuzz with conversations on what had just transpired. A pool was immediately started with bets as to whether or not Meghan and Michael would make it to the hospital, and a round of drinks on the house was ordered by an anxious grandfather-to-be.

A harried and bewildered Lucy rushed in on the pandemonium, and to her repeated inquiries as to what was happening, she got at least half a dozen different versions of the facts. However, they'd all come to the same conclusion. Meghan was about to deliver.

"I knew I shouldn't have stopped," she said, as she grabbed up her purse and coat again. "I ran into an old friend at the airport and she insisted we stop for coffee and catch up on each other's lives," she explained, as she finished fastening up the front of her lightweight coat. She turned and headed toward the private rear entrance at the back of the pub. "I feel just awful. I should have been here." Then she disappeared through the door.

Seconds later she reappeared, a sly, knowing smile on her face.

"On second thought," she confided to anyone listening, as she took a place at the bar beside Connie, "Who needs a fifth wheel at a time like this? The second round is on me, Pop."

Michael, in his frenzy, carried Meghan through the emergency doors at the hospital, shouting, "We're having our baby now," between calm, soothing instructions to Meghan.

Meghan took little comfort from his words. All the way to the hospital, he'd punctuated the Lamaze exercises with "I love you, Meghan," and "Everything'll be fine, darlin'." Oh, she knew he was well intentioned, but it wasn't his body trying to turn itself inside out to deliver this baby. She was worried about the baby.

How much more of this could the infant take? What if something was wrong? The book had said "very painful," not excruciating. It said labor could last anywhere from twelve to twenty-four hours and came in gradual stages. If this was the beginning, she'd never last to see the end of it. If this was indeed transition and it was all nearly over, hadn't it happened quicker than it should have? Was something wrong? Would her baby survive?

In addition to asking herself every age-old question asked by every laboring mother since the beginning of all time, Meghan was trying to focus on enduring each contraction as it came, bearing each intense pain until the darkness faded and the world came back into focus.

Michael had been asked to leave while Meghan was examined and prepared for delivery. The nurse told him to change into "delivery garb," which consisted of a way-too-small green gown, paper overshoes for his boots, and a paper hat no self-respecting cowboy would be caught dead in, except maybe if he were about to have a baby.

Back at Meghan's side he found her more and more upset. The intensity of the pain and her ever-increasing fear were leading her into a state of panic. She was like someone he'd never met before. His attempt to rub her aching muscles was met with a growl and a warning to keep his damned hands to himself. At one point she reached out and grabbed the front of his shirt with both hands and ordered him, through gnashing teeth, to get her something for the pain because his stupid breathing exercises were "a crock." If Michael hadn't been so worried about her, he might have been embarrassed.

It was about then that a short man with fuzzy gray hair and spectacles waltzed into the room with a piece of paper and a small black book in his hands.

"This is turning out to be quite a day for you two," he said in a thin, reedy voice, as he stood grinning at the overwrought parents-to-be.

"You damned well better be a doctor," Meghan told him bluntly.

The little man frowned and turned to Michael, hoping for a better reception.

"Well?" Michael boomed. "You're not the man who was here before, so who the hell are you?"

"I'm Judge Thaddeus Murphy. I've come to perform the nuptials," he explained, wondering if he'd wandered into the wrong room.

"What nuptials?" Meghan and Michael asked together.

Thad Murphy had sat on the bench for almost thirty years. In that time he'd only performed one other of these delivery-room weddings and had often wondered about the ethics of it as neither partner appeared to be in a sound state of mind under the circumstances. Such was the case here, but he was now considerably older and wiser.

"Are you Mary Meghan Shay?" he asked.

"Yes," she answered a little indignantly.

"And are you Michael James Ramsey?"

"Yes," was Michael's tentative answer.

"Do you two want to be married?" the judge asked solemnly.

"Yes," they both said automatically.

"That's good enough for me," the fuzzy-headed man declared. "Sign here, and you're tethered together forever," he waxed poetically.

Both men waited for Meghan's next contraction to pass, then smiled as each other while she and her nurse signed the paper; one as the bride, and the other as her witness.

Fifteen minutes later, Meghan and Michael watched the birth of their child, heard its angry wail, and all was calm again, contented and loving. The nurses and doctor congratulated Michael and met the real Meghan Shay Ramsey for the first time, adorable and charming and back to being herself.

• • •

Several hours later a glowing, if somewhat weary Meghan held court in her hospital room. Enthroned in crisp white sheets and propped with pillows, she smiled radiantly at her devoted subjects, as her nurse finished her ministrations.

"Yours is one delivery we won't soon forget," the nurse teased Meghan with a wink. "What a day," she said, as she left the room.

"She can say that again," Michael agreed, grinning broadly. "It can't be every day they help deliver a baby and witness a wedding in the same hour."

Everyone chuckled in unison, recalling with amused relief the events of the day.

"I still want to know where the judge came from," Meghan pondered aloud.

All eyes turned to Sean Shay, who gave a careless shrug before delivering his simple explanation. "Judges aren't as sober as most people think, and I haven't been standin' behind that bar for the last thirty years for nothing. I just called in a couple markers and got a few strings pulled to get the blood tests and waiting time waived by Judge Murphy. It was the least I could do for my first grandchild, considering the way you two were bungling everything. I've never heard such a ridiculous story," he said, shaking his head in wry amusement.

Meghan lowered her eyes. "I did bungle things, didn't I?" she uttered remorsefully.

"No more than I did," whispered Michael, as he placed an adoring kiss at her temple. "Besides," he added in more normal tones, "I thought we decided this was all meant to happen. We were simply playing out our parts in the divine design of things . . . including that first night. Lord knows, no mere mortal could have staged this and still come out with a happy ending." He laughed from deep in his chest. He bent slightly to take Meghan's hand in his. Their gazes met and they smiled their mutual happiness and contentment, silently repledging their devotion to one another.

"Mr. and Mrs. Ramsey?" came the nurse's voice from the doorway. "Your daughter wishes to join this party."

The newest member of the Shay-Ramsey clan was delivered into her mother's arms and held lovingly. Grandfather, uncles, godmother, and parents alike oohed and ahhed over her beauty and perfection.

"We're saving all the yellow blankets in the nursery for her," the nurse noted, then explained, "The pink ones clash with that red hair of hers. You'll never be able to claim there was a mix-up at the hospital and you took home the wrong baby," she teased. "That one is most certainly yours."

Meghan beamed her pride and laughed good-naturedly.

"She certainly is," piped Lucy. Then she added, "And well worth all the trouble."

"Oh, yes," Meghan agreed, her voice filled with awe. Then looking from her daughter into the loving, proud eyes of her husband, she said, "Well worth it. But next time I think I'll do it in a more conventional manner."

Michael chuckled and placed a tender kiss on her brow. Giving her a menacing glance, he said, "Damn right, you will."

THE EDITOR'S CORNER

We sail into our LOVESWEPT summer with six couples who, at first glance, seem to be unlikely matches. What they all have in common, and the reason that everything works out in the end, is Cupid's arrow. When true love strikes, there's no turning back—not for Shawna and Parker, her fiance, who doesn't even remember that he's engaged; not for Annabella and Terry, who live in completely different worlds; not for Summer and Cabe, who can't forget their teenage love. Holly and Steven were never meant to fall in love—Holly was supposed to get a juicy story, not a marriage proposal, from the famous bachelor. And our last two couples for the month are probably the most unlikely matches of all—strangers thrown together for a night who can't resist Cupid's arrow and turn an evening of romance into a lifetime of love!

We're very pleased to introduce Susan Crose to you this month. With **THE BRASS RING**, she's making her debut as a LOVESWEPT author—and what a sparkling debut it is! Be on the lookout for the beautiful cover on this book—it's our first bride and groom in a long time!

THE BRASS RING, LOVESWEPT #264, opens on the eve of Shawna McGuire's and Parker Harrison's wedding day when it seems that nothing can mar their perfect joy and anticipation on becoming husband and wife. But there's a terrible accident, and Shawna is left waiting at the church. Shawna almost loses her man, but she never gives up, and finally they do get to say their vows. This is a story about falling in love with the same person twice, and what could be more romantic than that?

Joan Elliott Pickart's **THE ENCHANTING MISS ANNA-BELLA,** LOVESWEPT #265, is such an enchanting love story that I guarantee you won't want to put this book down. Miss Annabella is the librarian in Harmony, Oklahoma, and Terry Russell is a gorgeous, blue-eyed, ladykiller pilot who has returned to the tiny town to visit his folks. All the ladies in Harmony fantasize about handsome Terry Russell, but Annabella doesn't even know what a fantasy is! Annabella's a late bloomer, and Terry is the

(continued)

one who helps her to blossom. Terry sees the woman hidden inside, and he falls in love with her. Annabella discovers herself, and then she can return Terry's love. When that happens, it's a match made in heaven!

FLYNN'S FATE, by Patt Bucheister, LOVESWEPT #266, is another example of this author's skill in touching our emotions. Summer Roberts loves the small town life and doesn't trust Cabe Flynn, the city slicker who lives life in Chicago's fast lane. Cabe was her teenage heartthrob, but years ago he gave up on Clearview and on Summer. Now he's back to claim his legacy, and Summer finds she can't bear to spend time with him because he awakens a sweet, wild hunger in her. Cabe wants to explore the intense attraction between them; he won't ignore his growing desire. He knows his own mind, and he also knows that Summer is his destiny—and with moonlight sails and words of love, he shows her this truth.

In **MADE FOR EACH OTHER** by Doris Parmett, LOVESWEPT #267, it's our heroine Holly Anderson's job to get an exclusive interview from LA's most eligible bachelor. Steven Chadwick guards his privacy so Holly goes undercover to get the scoop. She has no problem getting to know the gorgeous millionaire—in fact, he becomes her best friend and constant companion. Steven is too wonderful for words, and too gorgeous to resist, and Holly knows she must come clean and risk ruining their relationship. When friendly hugs turn into sizzling embraces, Holly gives up her story to gain his love. Best friends become best lovers! Doris Parmett is able to juggle all the elements of this story and deliver a wonderfully entertaining read.

STRICTLY BUSINESS by Linda Cajio, LOVESWEPT #268, maybe should have been titled, "Strictly Monkey Business". That describes the opening scene where Jess Brannen and Nick Mikaris wake up in bed together, scarcely having set eyes on each other before! They are both victims of a practical joke.

Things go from bad to worse when Jess shows up for a job interview and finds Nick behind the desk. They can't seem to stay away from each other, and Nick can't

(continued)

forget his image of her in that satin slip! Jess keeps insisting that she won't mix business with pleasure, even when she has the pleasure of experiencing his wildfire kisses. She doth protest too much—and finally her "no" becomes a "yes." This is Linda Cajio's sixth book for LOVESWEPT, and I know I speak for all your fans when I say, "Keep these wonderful stories coming, Linda!"

One of your favorite LOVESWEPT authors, Helen Mittermeyer, has a new book this month, and it's provocatively—and appropriately!—titled **ABLAZE**, LOVESWEPT #269. Heller Blane is a stunning blond actress working double shifts because she's desperately in need of funds. But is she desperate enough to accept $10,000 from a mysterious stranger *just* to have dinner with him? Conrad Wendell is dangerously appealing, and Heller is drawn to him. When their passionate night is over, she makes her escape, but Conrad cannot forget her. He's fallen in love with his vanished siren—she touched his soul—and he won't be happy until she's in his arms again. Thank you, Helen, for a new LOVESWEPT. **ABLAZE** has set our hearts on fire!

The HOMETOWN HUNK CONTEST is coming! We promised you entry blanks this month, but due to scheduling changes, the contest will officially begin next month. Just keep your eyes open for the magnificent men in your own hometown, then learn how to enter our HOMETOWN HUNK CONTEST *next month*.

Happy reading!

Sincerely,

Carolyn Nichols

Carolyn Nichols
    Editor
LOVESWEPT
Bantam Books
666 Fifth Avenue
New York, NY 10103